It's All Inside

How to Discover That Everything You Need is Within Your Reach

Kendrick Scott, M.S.

For information on special discounts for bulk purchases contact:

Kendrick Scott & Associates Communications Company, LLC
ph (850)-997-4686 • fx (850)-997-2113 • toll free (877)-813-0655

ISBN 978-1-4507-1786-151500

About the Author

"He makes an excellent impression the first time you meet him… he was a model student and player… I see him one day as Speaker of the House… he was great for our program… he has always had the ability to inspire and motivate others to reach for higher goals… not only does he have a powerful message and story to tell, he is great at delivering that message… you will be inspired to do and be more."

-Bobby Bowden
Head Coach, Florida State University

"His work ethic and leadership skills made him a person that was respected and looked up to by his teammates as well as the coaching staff… he is a very gifted person."

-Mark Richt
Head Coach, University of Georgia

"Ever since I've known him he has been an inspiration for me… when I had my difficult times his words were motivating and inspiring… he has never had any personal agenda, only to see me succeed… he was there to encourage me and help me get through those tough times."

-Anquan Bolden
Arizona Cardinals
2003 NFL Offensive Rookie of the Year

"There has not been anyone that has earned the respect from his teammates and his coaches like he has since I've been at Florida State."

-Clint Purvis
Florida State Team Chaplain 1989 – present

"In twenty-nine years there have been certain players that came through the program that have had what I call "IT"... that thing that made this program what it is... he is one of those players."

-Jim Gladden
Former FSU Assistant Head Coach

"He has a true gift and a real talent for speaking."

-Dave Van Halanger
University of Georgia, Director of Strength and Conditioning

"Ever since I've known him he has been great, and he still is... he is just an all around great person."

-Peter Warrick
Two-time Consensus All-American
Fourth Overall Pick in the NFL Draft

"He's the first person that comes to mind when I think of people who made Florida State successful during their run as Team of the Decade."

-Daryl Bush
Grid Iron Greats Interview

"His speech during the awards banquet was really inspirational... I am still moved by what he had to say."

-Unknown Fan
National Championship Reunion

Contents

Dedication

This book is dedicated to my little brother, Marvin Scott, who transitioned on April 3, 2000. He was a model student, wonderful brother, great son, and role model. His love for his family, friends, and church is unmatched. We all truly miss him and he will forever be in our hearts.

Acknowledgements

I would like to thank my parents, Evangelists Mr. and Mrs. Scott. They have been a source of inspiration for me my entire life. They are the reason for any level of success that I have and that I will ever attain. They gave us the best gift imaginable and that was teaching us to have faith and belief in Jesus Christ. I could not have completed this project or any other project without them in my life.

I would also like to thank my wife Felisha for allowing me to spend the time necessary to go after my dreams. I would like to thank my babies K.J. and Kennedy, for giving me a new meaning to life. I would like to thank my brothers and sister, Robert, Fran, and Monica, who have always challenged me to do more and reach for higher goals in life. I am proud to say that we have always done our best to look out for each other in any way we could just as our parents taught us. I would also like to thank their wives and my nieces and nephew: Valerie, Jakira, Robert Jr., Kari, Leslie, Alexis, and Alivia. I would also like to thank my goddaughter Latayvia for her continued support in everything.

I would like to give a special thanks to the entire True Gospel Mission Church family for their prayers in this and all my endeavors.

I would also like to thank Drs. Fred Seamon, Stephanie Powell-Hankerson, and Clarassia West- White for their helpful insight and direction in completing this project.

Preface

What are you searching for in life? Is it money, love, a thriving career or business, better relationships, happiness, or simply peace of mind? Whatever it is you are searching for, you must realize that it is all within your reach. Have you ever said to yourself, "If I had known then what I know now?" When you speak these words, what you are saying is that you wish you had recognized the opportunity that was before you. Literally, all your dreams and aspirations were only a decision away. The difference between people who are successful and those who are not is that successful people take advantage of the opportunities before them.

This book is about helping you to never miss an opportunity again. It will show you that everything that you need or want is all within your reach. After reading this book, you will be able to see the opportunities and make the right decisions.

I know that you have missed opportunities in the past; this is true for all of us. However, what you must understand is that you can still have everything that you want. It is all up to you. You do not have to spend a fortune, sacrifice your soul, or relinquish yourself to search for it. All you need to do is walk into the understanding that you already have everything that you need, in order to get anything that you want. Think for a second about a baby boy who realizes that his legs are for walking. Once he understands the concept and acts accordingly, then you are hard-pressed to make him sit down. A girl learning to swim further illustrates this point. She does not have to grow extra body parts in order to swim. She only has to come to the understanding that she is equipped with everything she needs, and then she can act accordingly.

This understanding has nothing to do with your sex, race, size, past, family history, the place you are from, or your age. People have accepted this understanding, even in their eighties and nineties, and have fulfilled lifelong dreams of wealth, happiness, and spiritual abundance. Your task will be accepting and walking into this understanding.

You should read this book with someone you trust and respect, and you should have him or her help you see what you have been missing. Many times, we cannot see within ourselves what we actually possess. We need help from others.

If you have everything that you want, then this book is not for you. Put it down; go and live your wonderful life. However, if you are looking to improve in some area of your life, you should read on because the answers lie within.

I have never been committed to reading one book at a time from cover to cover. Because I have a short attention span, I like reading more than one book at a time. Thus, this book is ideal for procrastinators, those who can't focus, and those who have never been able to commit to anything in their lives. It is perfect for those who may write a to-do list and arrive at their destination only to realize that they left the list at home.

Have you quit your bad habits hundreds of times? Have you given up on goals before you started reaching for them? If your answer is even partially yes to either of these questions, then you should keep reading. You will discover truths about yourself. Keep a count of the, "Ah hah" moments.

After reading this book, you will be ready to face whatever challenges may come your way. You will recognize that the past is over. Here, you are asked to use those past experiences only to help yourself presently and in the future. You will discover how to bring out the best in yourself in order for your career to blast-off and your relationships to improve, and then you can become the person you have dreamt of becoming.

Maybe you will not be inclined to read it from start to finish. As my freshman composition professor would say, "So what?" Do not feel guilty thumbing through the chapters. They consist of short methods, stories, gems, anecdotes, messages, quotes, movie dialogues, ideas, axioms, and analogies, so that you can do just that. Take from it what you need. Get from it what you want. Be blessed. I truly want you to have a wonderful life.

Foreword

Two times Kendrick Scott started at the bottom and finished at the top. One involved his football career at Florida State University, and the second involved his personal life after football. You cannot develop character if your life is rich from the top and always rosy. Somehow, you must start low and work your way to the top.

Kendrick enrolled at Florida State after graduating from Chiefland High School. I spoke at the Chiefland High School Senior Football banquet, where I first met Kendrick. Though he did not seem a Division I prospect, there was something about his enthusiasm that attracted me. I invited him to come to Florida State and come out for the football team as a preferred walk-on. Preferred, meaning he would receive special, but not monetary privileges until he proved himself. Through much hard work through his play, determination, and leadership, he proved that he belonged and earned a scholarship. Kendrick made the All ACC Academic Honor Roll three times. He was voted permanent team captain, along with Zack Crockett and Derrick Brooks. He also excelled in the classroom, enrolling in graduate school during his senior year and earning his Master's Degree.

FSU won the National Title in 1993. Kendrick, the rest of the team, and the coaches were honored by an invite to the White House to meet President Bill Clinton.

Kendrick also became a spokesman for the team on several occasions. He was one of the keynote speakers at the Sugar Bowl F.C.A. Breakfast. He was also asked by FSU's coaching staff to give the Captain's Address at the Annual Award's Banquet.

After leaving Florida State, Kendrick sank to what he calls the lowest point of his life. He slept in his car on occasion and found himself roaming the streets, searching for work alongside addicts of all kinds. He later committed to helping himself by studying the Bible and reading loads of self-help materials.

Kendrick's mission now is to teach others how they can use the resources that are all around and in front of them, to rise from the bottom to the top as he has had to do.

Kendrick's goal in this book is to inspire those who read it to realize that they are the masters of their fate. In it, he effectively illustrates that each person decides what he or she will become.

You will not only gain immeasurable knowledge but you will also enjoy reading this book.

Bobby Bowden
Head Football Coach
Florida State University

Introduction

A lot of people wander through their lives searching for clues that they hope will set them on the correct path to prosperity in their personal and professional lives. Usually it is not until it is too late that they realize what they have been looking for was in their grasp all along. The opportunities were not recognized and consequently not seized upon when they were presented. This book is geared towards helping people never to miss out on opportunities again. It will serve as a wake-up call to show each individual that he or she is the master of his or her own fate. It proves that you will come in contact with everything you need, in order to get anything that you want.

Kendrick and I were both linebackers as teammates at Florida State University. He was a tenacious player who overcame tremendous odds to become one of the team's leaders. During our senior year we were both voted as Permanent Team Captains. It's one of the highest honors bestowed on a player, because it's voted on by your teammates. Through this selection your peers are exhibiting confidence in you, that you are the person they want representing and leading them, on and off the field.

I have had the pleasure of hearing him speak at various times. He has always seemed to have wisdom and knowledge beyond his years. His words and the way he delivers them have always been very motivating and inspiring.

I was excited to learn that he had put all of his years of self-study, wisdom, and mastery of personal development, in a book.

If you are an individual, team, business, or organization, you will benefit greatly from the information contained herein. He reminds you that you are responsible for your life. God has equipped you with everything that you need to become the person you've dreamed of being. It is up to you to tap into the resources that you have and that are all around you. I'm also a strong believer in his perspective that if God is not a part of your success plan, that you will never totally be what you could or should be. However, your actions must match your desire, belief, and faith.

I have taken this approach with me in my personal and professional life. In 1995 I was fortunate to be selected in the first round of the NFL draft by the Tampa Bay Buccaneers. When I arrived in Tampa there was a sentiment that winning a Super Bowl was virtually impossible. As the years went by players like myself, Warren Sapp, John Lynch, Mike Alstott, Ronde Barber, and others, along with the coaching staff, including Coaches Tony Dungy, Monte Kiffin, and eventually Jon Gruden, all continued to believe and work toward turning the entire organization around. In effect with our positive mental attitudes, determination, hard work, and support of some great fans, we became Super Bowl XXX VII Champions. Not only did we win, but the sentiments of the organization, players, and fans, changed whereby people expected us to be Super Bowl contenders each year.

Whether you are looking to improve your physical appearance, make more money, expand your business, have better relationships, or become more spiritual, it is covered in this book. You will find the answers that you have been searching for in the chapters ahead. If you would digest the lessons that have been outlined in this book, you will invariably discover what you have been missing in your life.

Kendrick has eloquently put into words most of what I have been practicing all of my life. That is, that hard work, perseverance, dedication, and faith, will make you a champion in everything you do. I will now take some of the additional knowledge that I have learned after reading it, and apply it in my personal and professional life of sports, as well as my future business endeavors. It is a must-read for any person, team, business, or organization trying to get ahead and become successful.

Derrick Brooks
Nine-Time All Pro
Eleven-Time Pro Bowl Selection
AP NFL Defensive Player of the Year in 2002
Super Bowl XXX VII Champion

Revelation 23:13

"I am Alpha and Omega, the beginning and the end, the first and the last."

Exodus 34:14, "For thou shalt worship no other god: for the LORD, whose name is Jealous, is a jealous God."

God has to be at the start of everything you do. People usually say God is at the center of their lives. That is fine if that is where you begin your life. The problem is that most people do not start their lives from the center out. They start their lives from the outside in (see diagram 1.1).

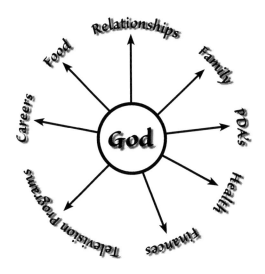

As in the diagram, we usually have so much around God that we can't get to him.

Before anything starts, we must know where and how it begins. Genesis 1:27 reads, "God created man in his own image, in the image of God created he him; male and female created he them." Before we can do and be more, we must start our lives correctly. Many people have other gods, but they do not realize it. Their kids, computers, careers, television programs, food, sports teams, radio programs, the gym, PDAs, cell phones, iPods, houses, cars, and businesses are their gods. Some people feel that it is okay to obsess in many facets of their lives, but if you ask someone to recite scripture concerning the Creator and a spiritual purpose for their lives, you will be labeled a religious fanatic. But without God as a part of all of our lives, we will never be what we could or should be.

Some people begin their careers because they are looking for money, prestige, and power among other things. Let me be the first to tell you, in case you didn't know, you can have a rewarding career, money in the bank, and customers lined up at your door, but with each of these you may also have accumulated enough stress to send you to the state mental institution.

Some people start their exercise and diet programs because they want to be thin or feel accepted. Wrong! What you should do is ask God to help you with how you look and feel about yourself. We are not all shaped alike. We cannot all be skinny, have long hair, and have perfect frames. We all have differences, but that does not mean that we should never exercise, bathe, and put on decent clothes. It does mean, however, that we must learn to accept and appreciate ourselves first. I have known many people who have had their stomachs stapled or undergone gastric bypass surgery and lost one hundred or more pounds, but also lost their spirit in the process.

There are people who begin relationships and later get married because they are in love. Wrong again! For a great deal of people, even love will not get them past the fact that their spouse leaves his toenail clippings on the kitchen table, or that it sounds like JFK airport when he is asleep, or that she places the toilet paper roll in the position from which a person has to pull it from the top rather than from the bottom. The fact is that half of all first marriages, two-thirds of all second marriages, and three-quarters of all third marriages end in divorce. It is evident that love will not keep people together, not to mention other reasons for getting married, such as unplanned pregnancy, financial stability, and peer pressure. How many people do you know who are in horrible relationships? How many say that they are only in it for the kids or financial support? How many of these people are lonely, feel unworthy, and unloved? Matthew 19:6 reads, "What God has put together, let no man put asunder." Billy Graham said that true love is between a man, a woman, and God. God should be first in any and all of your relationships. This will make not only for a better relationship, but will also help you to see your spouse as God sees them. Many times in relationships, our vision is so clouded with our own idiosyncrasies that we can't see ourselves as God sees us. Consequently, we cannot see others as God sees them either.

You can have a great career, be skinny as a rail, find the person you think is right for you, be loved and adored by millions, and still feel empty and lonely. Actually, you may even feel emptier than you did before you acquired your job, figure, mate, and adoring fans.

Abd-ar-Rahman was considered the greatest and most successful of the princes of the Umayyad dynasty. He ruled from

912-961. He came to power at the age of twenty-two and ruled for half of a century. Outwardly, he appeared to be a successful and contented man, yet his internal struggles outweighed any success he had gained. This is evident in a statement made at the end of his reign,

> *"I have now reigned about 50 years in victory or peace, beloved by my subjects, dreaded by my enemies, and respected by my allies. Riches and honors, power and pleasure, have waited on neither my call, nor does any earthly blessing appear to have been wanting to my felicity. In this situation, I have diligently numbered the days of pure and genuine happiness that have fallen to my lot. They amount to 14. O, men place not thy confidence in this presence world."*

What an interesting statement for a man of his caliber and position. No one would have ever imagined that being a successful ruler for all of those years would have only brought fourteen days of happiness!

I am not anti-money, anti-happiness, or anti-fame. In fact, I happen to think that money is very important, and the remainder of this book speaks about getting more out of life than you already have. Money is ranked highly on my list because whatever you are doing, or want to do, will cost money, i.e., entertaining, driving, sleeping, eating, etc. I say get all the money you want without hurting others, give away more than your fair share, and help as many people as you can, and you will start your journey toward the fulfillment of your purpose in life. I strongly believe in what Paul wrote to Gaius in 3 John 1:2, "I wish above all things that you may prosper and be in health even as thy soul prospers." However, if God is not a part of your success plan, then in the end, you will find yourself feeling empty, alone, and unworthy.

It has often been said that you can have things as long as things do not have you. Dr. Mike Murdock said that God would not create a world in which he would not be needed. Billionaire oil magnate John D. Rockefeller, once the richest man in the world, was once asked, "How much money do you need?" He replied, "Just a little bit more than what I have." That is the attitude of most people. They feel as long as they gain quantity in life that it will someday equate to a better quality of life. This could not be further from the truth. A long list of movie stars, athletes, entertainers, and politicians have quantity in life, but when it comes to quality, they suffer so much that they single-handedly keep rehabilitation centers in business.

Marilyn Monroe was once the most sought after woman in the world, and to this day remains one of the most intriguing. She had what most people only dream of having. She was rich, famous, beautiful, influential, and seemed to have life in the palms of her hands. However, toward the end of her life she battled depression like a person who was friendless and didn't have a dime, and it is widely believed that she took her own life because of it.

You can't think that what you become or gain will give you

ultimate peace, especially if God does not hold His proper place in your acquisitions, or in who you become. However, when you start every aspect of your life for the right reason, and you ask God to not only direct you, but to make you a vessel for him, you will see your life come into focus. Those incomplete tasks become completions. You start to feel great about yourself and the journey you are embarking on. You gain the confidence that you need to be successful. The right people gravitate towards you. Plans, goals, and dreams that were not in your reach before, start to become evident. You begin to walk into the understanding that you have everything that you need. Your face glows, and your heart fills with kindness in everything you do. You start to believe in yourself and in others more than you ever have before. Your thoughts become pure. Your worries disappear. You are less likely to be associated with conflict. Joel Osteen says, "It's important to program your mind for success. That won't happen automatically. Each day you must choose to live with an attitude that expects good things to happen to you."

Here is an affirmation that you should say each day:

Lord, make me a vessel for you today. Let me plan my life today according to the dreams and goals that you have for me. I recognize that everything starts and ends with you. It is by you and only you that I am here today. I ask for your help in leading and guiding me this day. Everything that I am and will ever be is because of you. I fully submit myself to you and your will. It is through you that everything in and outside of life emanates. Without your presence and direction I realize that it does not matter what I do or achieve. Without you, I am not anything. I am grateful for what is and thankful for what is to come. I take nothing for granted. I ask you to forgive me of the transgressions that I made against you, others, and myself. Help me to start each day and each task with you in mind.

STOP! Before you read any further, reread the affirmation.

Chapter 2: The Choices You Make

"What we call the secret of happiness is no more a secret than our willingness to choose life."

-Leo Buscaglia

I had generally never been a fan of The Oprah Winfrey Show. I based my conclusions on what I thought and never took the time to watch the show or to see what she was about. I was on a business trip sitting in my hotel room and saw what appeared to be Oprah on at an odd time. It was Oprah after the Show. I do not remember who the guests were, but I watched as she poured her heart into her work after all the prime-time cameras were turned away. I gained a new respect for her and what she did.

Sometime later, I was doing some channel surfing when the television landed on one of those celebrity-gossip news programs. I watched as a reporter interviewed Oprah before she walked into an awards show. He asked her about her fame, success, and secrets for becoming successful. She turned to him, in an off-the-cuff kind of way, and said, "It's the choices that you make that determine the dreams that you have." At first, I must admit, I did not think much of that statement, but as time went on, I could not remove it from my mind. It started to pierce my brain with an ever-increasing sharpness that barred me from thinking of anything else. As images of my life began to flash in my mind, I started to ponder the choices that I had made, and it became penetratingly clear that those choices had indeed determined where I was in life.

I then thought about Oprah. Her parents were merely teenagers when she was born. Her mother was a maid and her father was a serviceman. She had meager beginnings, living with her grandmother until age six and then moving to the inner city of Milwaukee, Wisconsin to live with her mother. During that stay, family members often molested her. She became a very rebellious teenager, due in part to the abuse that she had suffered. She was sent to a juvenile detention home at the age of thirteen, only to be denied admission because all the beds were filled. Her life started to turn around when she was sent to live with her father in Nashville, Tennessee. He was a strict disciplinarian who demanded high morals and good grades.

She could have made excuses for all of the reasons why she should have failed. She could have accepted welfare checks, relied on the government to take care of her, or chosen some mediocre employment opportunity to help her to just get by. She had plenty of reasons to live in and below mediocrity, yet she chose a different way of life. She made some choices that placed her as arguably the wealthiest and most influential woman in history. Choices that she made took her from poverty to billionaire-wealth, and made her the owner of a production company and the creator of a brand. Her choices took her from the slums in Milwaukee to high-rise condominiums all over the world. She used the issues of her life as stepping stones to make choices that would take her from where she had been to where she wanted to go.

After thinking about her life, I pondered her statement again. What if some of my decisions had been different? Where would I have been and what would I have being doing? What are some of the choices that you have made in your life? Can you see a correlation between the choices that you have made and the dreams that you have?

Most people think about the choices that they have made and can only cry. Stephen R. Covey said, "While we are free to choose our actions, we are not free to choose the consequences of our actions."

I was watching Dr. Phil's television show as he was counseling a young woman and her husband. The woman suffered from alcoholism and because of her problems, the couple's finances, relationship, and subsequently their marriage, were in trouble. As the interview proceeded, Dr. Phil began grilling her. She began to cry saying, "But, but I'm a good person, I'm not a bad person." Dr. Phil said to her, "You're not a good or a bad person, you're just a person. What makes you good or bad are the choices that you make."

You see, none of us are born winners or losers; we are born choosers. For many people, their dreams are not dreams, they are nightmares. There are people who are in bad relationships, have terrible careers, and have failing health all because of the choices that they have made. I believe that the one great thing that we are blessed with is the free will to do whatever we want. However, the one thing that we are cursed with is the free will to do whatever we want. Deepak Chopra said, "The physical world, including our bodies, is a response of the observer. We create our bodies as we create the experience of our world."

Your choices determine where you are and what you will be, so you must start making better choices today. Do not sit around thinking about the choices that you have made and allow those thoughts to eat away at the fabric of your life. Do not read this and dig yourself a deeper hole of resentment by saying that you only make bad decisions, choose the wrong friends, jobs, and the like. Do not start saying to yourself that you are a loser because of the choices and decisions that you have made. You must realize that you need to take responsibility for your actions and know that you can do something to change your situation. You must understand that the past is over and it does not equal the future. You must say to yourself that the choices you make from this point forward will determine the dreams that you will later experience. You must say to yourself that you will not miss opportunities in your life because of fear, self-doubt, and hopelessness. It is possible to start over and make better choices. You should remind yourself that the choices you make today will determine the dreams that become your reality tomorrow.

Walls

Ronald Reagan said, "There are no constraints to the human mind, no walls around the human spirit, no barriers to our progress, except for those we ourselves erect."

You should be careful not to allow the choices of your past to create barricades to your future. We all have had negative and positive affirmations in our lives. The problem comes when we choose to focus on those negative affirmations rather than the positive.

The negative affirmations act as walls that limit your possibilities. These walls represent limiting beliefs that convince you that you cannot accomplish your goals and dreams. These are walls that we ourselves have built or that others have built for us.

There are walls of all kinds. Some walls are built because of beliefs about our intellect. Other walls are built because of the negative thoughts we have about our appearance: we either think that we are too skinny or too fat. We believe that we are too tall or too short. Early in our lives, our friends, parents, teachers, family members, and the media help us build these walls. We are constantly reminded of who we are not instead of who we are, making it easier to focus on negative messages. The walls in our lives must be torn down before we can travel to new destinations and new heights. You cannot become great at what you do or who you are if you are living behind walls.

From 1949 until 1961, it was estimated that more than 2.5 million East Germans fled to West Berlin. People from the East German state wanted to escape its repressive and oppressive communist system. The overall quality of life was better in the West than in the East. East Germany started to lose too many skilled workers, thus its government decided to prevent people from escaping to the West by closing the border and constructing a wall.

In a speech to the people of West Berlin, President Ronald Reagan, promoting openness and freedom said, "We in the West stand ready to cooperate with the East to promote true openness, to break down barriers that separate people, to create a safe, freer world… General Secretary Gorbachev, if you seek peace, if you seek prosperity… come here to this gate… tear down this wall."

After his speech, "tear down this wall" was all Americans heard. Much like the East Germans who wanted to escape to a better life in West Berlin, they could not do so freely until a wall was torn down.

In the movie Instinct, Ethan Powell (Anthony Hopkins) is a very intelligent primatologist, who has been jailed for murders that were committed in the Rwandan jungles where he spent many years studying the mountain gorillas. Psychiatrist Theo Caulder (Cuba Gooding, Jr.) is assigned his case to study and crack the mysterious mind of Mr. Powell. It is not known if Theo ever gets through to him, but in the end, a letter by Ethan to Theo reads in part, "Freedom is not just a dream. It exists on the other side of those fences that we create for ourselves." Just like Ethan, you will never gain freedom unless you walk into the understanding that freedom is just over the fence or around the wall you have created. Once you understand that your freedom is just on the other side, you will stop at nothing to get through and over the barriers.

How many walls and fences have you created for yourself? How many issues in your past have you allowed to become a barrier for you because you thought you that they made you inadequate? Proverbs 23:7 reads, "As he thinketh in his heart so is he." James Allen wrote, "Man is literally what he thinks… he is made or unmade by himself. By the right choice, he ascends. As a being of power, intelligence, and love, and the lord of his own thoughts, he holds the key to every situation."

I have always wanted to act, to be on television and in the movies. In my mind, I did not possess "the look" that Hollywood desired. I grew up without cable television, so my world-view was limited. I did not see very many people who I felt looked like me on television. I later learned of Sidney Poitier and his accomplishments on the big screen. By that time, I had already built a wall for myself.

I had always performed well in plays in grade school. My fifth grade teacher chose me to play the part of Santa Claus in a fifth grade play, which was a big deal considering I am as far from resembling a traditional Santa Claus as one could imagine. I was chosen as best actor of my high school drama class and I was told by many that I should at least give acting a shot. However, the negative connotation that I held about myself outweighed any talent my teachers or peers thought I had. I made the choice to focus on the wrong message. I have never been to an audition, taken any higher level acting classes, been to any screenings, or hired an agent, nor do I have a portfolio or a bio page on the Internet. The truth is, I created this wall for myself and I chose not to go over or around it.

The only thing worse than creating walls for yourself, is allowing others to build walls for you. It could be someone who tells you that you are just like your father and you will never amount to anything, or it could be an abusive spouse who says that you are too ugly for anyone to love. It could be a teacher, coach, or someone you look up to, who tells you you do not have what it takes to succeed. As events take place in our lives, we begin to believe in these walls.

Statements like these are made: "I knew he was right when he said that I would not amount to anything." "My husband left me because I am ugly." "I am not smart enough and that is why I was passed up for that promotion." "I never thought that we were good enough to win; they have mounds more talent than us."

When these walls are built solid enough, you cannot see yourself ever getting through, around, or over them. You need to tear down these walls if you are going to ever move from neglect and regret to having a better life. You need to destroy these walls if success is to come.

These walls are blockades that not only keep us from moving on to successful places in our lives, but they keep us from even knowing that there is a better life out there.

When I left my hometown to attend college, I was afforded opportunities to visit other cities like New York, Miami, Dallas, and Atlanta. It was only then that I started to realize that another world existed. In my opinion, people hardly ever left my hometown because they did not understand that there was something more to the world than their own lives. The same rings true for people in other cities, whether big or small. If people never venture outside of their neighborhoods, they cannot possibly know that the world is bigger than their backyards. In other words, the walls in their lives become a prison; these walls trap them in their current positions. It is like a woman who has been married and divorced five times; she sees a couple kissing in the park and says to herself that love is not real or that it does not last. She does not believe in love because of her past relationships. She should tear those walls down if she is ever to have a lasting, loving relationship.

These walls cannot be there when you go to job interviews. You cannot carry your walls with you when you are trying to sell your product or sponsor a person in your business. You cannot have walls when you are going to read for a part in a movie. You cannot have walls when you are trying out for a roster spot on a football team. Those walls must be destroyed before you attempt to go from the minor league to the majors. You cannot have walls when you are teeing off on your last golf hole for the victory. You cannot have walls when you go out on a date with the man or woman of your dreams. You cannot have walls when writing a screenplay. Those walls must be gone before you decide to take your company public. Those walls must be knocked down when looking for an investor for your business. Those walls cannot be there when trying to secure a mortgage for a home. Get rid of the walls in your life and do not allow any more to be built.

Finding Your Niche

Once you tear down those walls, you will be better able to find your place in life. Sophia Loren said, "Getting ahead in a difficult profession requires avid faith in yourself. That is why some people with mediocre talent, but with great inner drive, go much further than people with vastly superior talent."

What are you good at? What is something that you would do for free if there were no financial gains? It is something that you do not mind putting time into. It is productive and legal.

There are people who get upset because they cannot "be like Mike." You should find the thing that you can do well and quickly become the Michael Jordan of your sport, hobby, or profession. There is no better example of this than when Michael Jackson and Michael Jordan teamed up to shoot a commercial. In the commercial, Michael Jordan, the greatest basketball player and possibly the greatest athlete of all time, and Michael Jackson, one of, if not the, greatest singers/entertainers of all time, tried to teach each other their respective craft. Michael Jordan was horrible at dancing and Michael Jackson looked as if he had never picked up a basketball in his life. It is rather evident that if Michael Jordan had tried to make his living dancing, he would have failed miserably. Similarly, Michael Jackson would have never made a dime playing basketball. Both would have had empty arenas and empty pockets if they switched professions. However, place them in Madison Square Garden, surround them with the same fans, give each his tool of the trade, a basketball to one and a microphone to the other, and you would get five MVP awards, nine All-Defensive first team honors, fourteen all-star appearances, seven straight and ten total scoring titles, six NBA championships, thirteen Grammy awards, the bestselling album of all time, thirteen number one singles, and 750 million records sold. **FIND YOUR NICHE!**

In finding your niche, you will ultimately find out who you are. It is usually never a good idea to emulate someone else. It does not matter how good the photocopier, it can never make the original copy. It may be close, but it will never be the real thing.

A bird and a rabbit were having a conversation. The rabbit said to the bird that he could imitate any animal that he wanted. The bird said to the rabbit, "Ok, sing like me." Sure enough after practicing a couple of days, the rabbit was singing like the bird. The bird said, "I'll bet you can't climb like a squirrel." The rabbit said, "I'll return in a couple of weeks." The rabbit came back a couple of weeks later and was climbing trees, jumping from branch to branch, up and down, across and over. The bird said, "That is amazing. If you perform this next feat, then you'll have to tell me your secret." The rabbit said, "Go ahead, try me." The bird said, "I'll bet you can't swim like a fish." The rabbit said, "Give me a month." He came back within a month, jumped into the lake, and started to swim. The rabbit swam across the lake and on his way back, he began doing the backstroke, bragging, telling the bird how well he could imitate anything, even singing on occasion, and had a great time. Just as he was about to arrive at his destination, a hawk mistook him for a fish, swooped down, scooped him up, and ate him. The moral of the story is: Do not try to be something you are not because even if you succeed you will eventually fail.

Find what you were put on the earth to do. Some people call it talent, others call it bliss. Either you work hard and become good at it or it is something that comes natural to you.

There are people who were born to do what they do, because they were born with certain interests. For instance, there are people who grow up with a passion for computers. Programming, building, and repairing computers fascinates them. One such person is Michael Dell, founder of Dell, Inc., who took his computer apart and put it back together at the age of sixteen. There are kids who grow up in mechanic shops. The sounds of engines running is like music to their soul. Their fascination and knowledge seems unmatched. They become mechanics, engineers, and designers. There are kids who can sing and dance at early ages. They grow up to be entertainers. Some kids cry if they do not get the chance to play with their doctor kits or model airplanes before bedtime. They grow up to become doctors and pilots. Others are athletically gifted. You put them on the football field or basketball court and it is as if they were born there. When you look back, you can say it was in them from the beginning.

Some people find their talent later on in life. For instance, the internet was not prevalent until only a few years ago. Today, however, there are people who have built companies and amassed fortunes online. Thus, through the internet, people have found their niche in newly developed technologies.

I am sorry, but your niche cannot be watching television, sleeping, or eating. Your niche is not playing fantasy football, shopping, or playing video and computer games. These are all fun activities that we enjoy, but you cannot spend all of your time participating in these activities.

Your niche can make you a living. It is something that you have found that makes you stand above the crowd. You should find your niche and act on it, and not someone else's. Barbara Walters is a great reporter/interviewer, but I would venture to guess that she would not make a great rapper or race-car driver, as she cannot even drive. If she had tried to make a living at either of these professions, she would have been considered a failure. However, place her in front of a warm body and she delivers. You only need to find one thing that you are good at doing. When you follow your dream with ferocious intent, you will either make it happen, or you will stumble onto your true calling.

Yes, it is true that some people are born with certain advantages. Some people are born on third base. Some are even born with ownership of the team. Some of us are not born with much at all; it can be said that we are born in the dugout. But if you have enough desire, it does not matter where you are born. If you want something and you follow it with your heart, you will be rewarded. Do not think that just because you are not where you want to be today that you will never get there.

An old Chinese proverb says," The journey of a thousand miles begins with a single step." I advise that before you take that step, you must first put on some shoes. People try so hard to get to where they want to be in life that they fail to realize that everything is a process. Your process may be different from someone else's, but you must still go through the process. It has nothing to do with how you feel or how bad you want something. You must go the way that you must go to get what you want. What has to be done has to be done. You may have all the ingredients for a cake, but it cannot make itself. The ingredients have to be mixed and the directions followed to get the desired results: an edible and tasty slice of cake. Of course, you should be in a hurry, but do not be so desperate that you forget that there is a process.

Our world revolves around instant gratification: we want everything now. We want it yesterday. No one wants to wait on anything. No one wants to take the time to do things right. This now-today-tomorrow-or-never attitude could cause irreparable damage for a lifetime. Do not be afraid to take some time and weigh all of your options or get a second opinion. There may be a better option than the one on the table. The lure of having your dream car today works against us in most cases. The salesperson uses the puppy-dog technique, which is often successful. He allows us to drive the car home; we buy the car based on our emotions rather than rational thinking. We listen to and agree to everything the salesperson tells us because we are not paying attention to the details. All we think about is how we will look when driving to our class reunion, relative's house, or the grocery store. We have totally lost connection with reality. Three months later, reality hits us in the face when our credit is dinged, the car is no good, the warranty is out, and the interest rate resembles our age. Slow down. A day is not a long enough amount of time to make a decision, nor is a week, or a month, in some cases. You do not have to be married by a certain age just because it was your childhood dream. If you are not with the right person, then the time is not right. For all those telling you to go forth, a thousand others will tell you the importance of waiting until the time is right. You need to be patient and conscientious in your quests.

Hobby Love

You should exhaust all of your abilities and talents on doing what you do, but you must distinguish between a hobby and a profession when searching for your niche. There are people spending time in what they believe are careers, but they are wasting time because their "careers" are really hobbies. If you often times come home and immediately head to the shed to grab your guitar and microphone, to sing and play without any intentions of ever performing in front of people, then you have yourself a hobby.

When I finished playing football in college, I wanted to test my skills as a free agent. I was injured three times on three different occasions on the days I was to start my training regime.

I realized that something or someone was trying to tell me something. This was not the path for my life. If I wanted to stay in the game, I was going to have to find another avenue, whether that was coaching, commentating, or just watching, but it was not going to be playing professionally.

Later I returned to my first passion, playing basketball. I was an avid player on many adult league teams, but I had to come to the realization that that was as far as I was going to go. I could not allow my hobby to affect my career aspirations, goals, or dreams. The problem lies not with the hobby, but in allowing the hobby to become a barrier between you and your future. If you are a writer, you will need an environment that facilitates your writing. If you are an internet marketer, you need to spend your time analyzing your site's statistics so you can best understand how to maximize its potential instead of surfing, gaming, or social networking.

If you cannot guard yourself from all the distractions, then what you have is a hobby. It does not matter what your aspirations are. Sometimes you just have to face the facts.

Some people feel that just because they love something they will be able to do it professionally. I have known several people who love to sing, but cannot hold a note. These people cannot hear themselves and the people who are around them are afraid to crush their dreams, unless of course they are Simon Cowell from American Idol. How many times have you seen people audition for the show who really believe they can sing but cannot, yet their parents and friends stand outside encouraging them?

You may never play Major League Baseball, be a classical pianist, track star, the next American Idol, or win the So You Think You Can Dance competition, but understand you were not put here to be a spectator and call or text in your vote either. You can do something else. There is another side to life than just sitting in the stands. So figure out what you can do and do it.

Make a Run at It

> *"If one advances confidently in the direction of their dreams and endeavors to lead a life which they have imagined they will meet with a success unexpected in common hours."*
> *-Henry David Thoreau*

You should give everything you have when making a serious run at fulfilling your passions. While on this journey, you should counsel and obtain opinions from several objective people you trust, and accept constructive criticism. You should be able to hear the truth but only allow it to positively affect you. I urge you to stay on the path to your dreams. You never know where it may lead. While following your passions, you may end up stumbling upon your true calling.

A walk-on football player at the University of Maryland chose not to make a career out of professional football. He instead started a little t-shirt company and asked some of the players that he befriended in college to wear them. They did, and with a great deal of hard work and determination, his company took off. In November 2005, at the release of its Initial Public Offering IPO, the stock had the second highest increase in share price ever for the first day of trading, debuting at thirteen dollars a share, and doubling at close to just over twenty-six dollars per share. On that day, his net worth shot to about $800 million dollars. The name of his "little t-shirt company" is Under Armour. Today, Kevin Plank does not care that he is not playing football.

A guy prospecting for gold in California decided that he was probably not going to find gold, so he decided to make a durable pair of pants for fellow prospectors. His name was Levi Strauss.

One day, a manager on a track team picked up a javelin and began to throw it. He was good. In fact, he had Olympic ability. However, before the dream could be realized, he suffered a career ending injury. After he could no longer compete, he decided to take some acting classes. He became pretty good at acting too, and portrayed such memorable characters as Little Joe Cartwright of *Bonanza*, Charles Ingalls of *Little House on the Prairie*, and Jonathan Smith of *Highway to Heaven*. His given name was Eugene Maurice Orowitz, but we know him today as the late Michael Landon.

What are you passionate about? Are there professional options associated with your passions? There may be something bigger and better for you around the corner that will make your previous plans look small in comparison. So stay encouraged and on the right path.

Chapter 3: Pay It Forward

"*The only difference between a rut and a grave is their dimensions.*"

-Ellen Glasgow

In the movie Pay It Forward, a class of young students is challenged to create something that might change the world. One of the students, Trevor, believes so much in the teacher and the assignment that he tries to accomplish its mission. He believes that he can truly change the world. He finally gets an idea. He calls it "Pay It Forward." "Pay It Forward" asks each person to do something for three other people that they cannot do for themselves. The people accepting the favor cannot in turn repay the person who gave it to them. They can only pay their favors forward to three new people.

During a scene in the movie, Trevor sees some bullies picking on a helpless little boy and quickly figures that helping the boy could be counted as one of his favors. He ultimately decides not to help the boy because he allows his fear to control his actions. Trevor continues his project and starts to encourage others to do the same. He is interviewed later at school about his popular project, which has caught the attention of the media. Later, while leaving the interview, he sees the bullies beating up on the little boy again. This time, however, Trevor stands up to the bullies. In the process, he is stabbed and killed. Although he never thinks that anything ever came of his project, there are millions of people who have been affected. Many of them show up to his home after his death to give a candlelight vigil. The movie ends playing excerpts of his voice. One of the things that he says is, "I guess it's hard for some people, who are so used to things the way they are, even if they're bad, to change, 'cause I guess they kind of give up and when they do everybody kinda loses."

When you do not continue on your journey, not only do you lose, but everyone else loses too. Sometimes you are the last grasp of hope for people in your family. You are the one they rely on. There are people who are watching your life; therefore, you should be careful, attentive, and aware of the fact that others are watching you. You may be able to change a person's life by spending time with him or her, having an honest conversation, giving some much-needed advice, expressing encouragement, or lending a listening ear.

Little Eyes upon You

"There are little eyes upon you and they're watching night and day. There are little ears that quickly take in every word you say. There are little hands all eager to do anything you do; and a little boy who's dreaming of the day he'll be like you. You're the little fellow's idol; you're the wisest of the wise. In his little mind about you, no suspicions ever rise. He believes in you devoutly, holds all that you say and do; He will say and do, in your way, when he's grown up like you. There's a wide-eyed little fellow who believes you're always right; and his eyes are always opened, and he watches day and night. You are setting an example every day in all you do, for the little boy who's waiting, to grow up to be like you."

-Author unknown

My little brother was killed in a car accident at the age of twenty. We often hear that God does not make mistakes and that he will never put more on us than we can bear. We often have read in Romans 8:28 that, "All things work together for good to those that love God, to those who are the called according to his purpose." But it sure is hard when the test comes and hits you in the face.

On the day of his passing, I watched my parents, who are Evangelists, as they maneuvered both naturally and spiritually. I must say that I did not question God, but I did stop talking to him for a while. I watched my parents as they never lost faith, which was comforting to me. They had just lost their youngest son to a premature death and they still were solid in their faith. I wanted to give up. I had many thoughts of taking my car over a bridge or driving it into a tree, but when I saw their dedication to what they had preached for years, it became easier for me to pull through. I needed their strength to survive. I am glad they did not give up because I would have. Then, we all would have lost.

There are people out there that only you can help. There are people out there that are waiting on you. You are their beacon of light. You are the only person that can give encouragement, help, and hope. They are secretly rooting for you. So keep doing what you are doing. You might be the person that can hire a friend at eight dollars an hour, just the amount needed to keep his or her family together. You may be able to give your church an extra $10,000 toward the mortgage. You may be the sibling who has to pay some unforeseen adult daycare expenses for your aging parents. Your life is not all about you. During a natural disaster, as we had with Hurricane Katrina, what if you had been able to pay for one hundred homes to be built? What type of impact would this have had? When you are tired, think about the big picture. When you are afraid of the business call, think about others who may be depending on you. They will appreciate what you have done, and all of the hard work, effort, coffee drinking, late nights, long meetings, conference calls, giving, etc., would have been worth it, not only for you, but for others also.

The Bible reads that it is better to give than to receive. What if you were known as a giver? People who hoard in order to get, continue to hoard when they get, because they think that is how they got what they got. Then they wonder why they stopped getting. People who give to get usually continue giving because they believe in the principal of giving; when you give it shall be given unto you. You will always get when you give. It has often been said that people give because they have, but the inverse is actually true; people have because they give. For the rich, it is easier to give money than it is to give time. For the poor, it is easier to give time than it is money. The key is to find some gifting balance in your life.

Mother Teresa, a former schoolteacher from Calcutta, India, was very bothered by the mass amounts of poverty in the world. She mentioned that she felt a calling from within, to not only help the poor, but to live with them. She said, "I was to leave the convent and help the poor while living among them."

Harriet Tubman was a slave who escaped the plantation and then led others to their freedom. Even though she was free, she went back and not only helped her family to gain their freedom, but also countless others who wanted theirs. After being a slave for so long and then experiencing freedom, she knew she had to share it. She said, "I had crossed the line. I was free, but there was no one to welcome me to the land of freedom. I was a stranger in a strange land." She believed that it was her responsibility to help others. She was so committed to her vision that she was willing to risk her own freedom and life to see her vision become reality.

I believe that it is everyone's responsibility to help someone else. We have all had help, whether it was in the form of a mentor, bank loan, gift, college fund, job, investor, or just an opportunity. No one gets to the podium without having anyone to thank. It was not escaping the plantation that made Harriet Tubman famous. She is famous for helping others to escape the plantation as well. It is good to do, but it is great to inspire.

Take some food to the shelter. Give some clothes to Goodwill. Volunteer with Habitat for Humanity. You should do something that will have a positive impact on others. I am sure that you will feel just as good as the people to whom you lend a hand.

Give Them Hope

> *"Never deprive someone of hope: it might be all they have."*
> *-H. Jackson Brown, Jr.*

In the movie Flight of the Phoenix, Captain Frank Towns (Dennis Quaid) and his crew are sent to shut down an unproductive oil rig in the Mongolian desert and fly the staff home. While on their way out of the desert, they encounter a sandstorm that forces them to crash-land. Frank makes the decision to wait on help and conserve resources instead of being proactive in an attempt to leave the desert. The crew becomes torn when one of its members believes that the plane can be rebuilt. James Lidell (Scott Michael Campbell), seemingly in protest, wanders off into the desert. Frank, concerned about the deterioration of the crew, sets out on a mission to find him and return him to the fold.

Upon finding him, Frank urges James to return with him. James explains to Frank that they should try to rebuild the plane. He says that he is not going to just sit there and die. James says, "I think a man only needs one thing in life and that is someone to love, and if you can't give him that, give him something to hope for, and if you can't give him that, give him something to do." Frank, inspired by James's speech, goes back to the wreckage and joins his crew in their endeavor to rebuild the plane. They ultimately accomplish their goal; they rebuild the plane and fly home safely.

Most of us just need something in which to believe or hope for. We need something to keep us going - whether it is a great idea, an invention, a fledgling music career, or a part-time business – something that helps us to believe that we have some chance for success. So you should keep believing, keep hoping, and keep trying. If you have any kind of ambition, then you should keep dreaming. You must dream until the day they throw the dirt on you. Do not allow your dreams to fade. Do not allow your ambitions to float away in a sea of disbelief. Do not let others steal your dream. Continue to do what you feel in your heart. For some of us, all we have to hold onto is a glimmer of hope, a ray of sunshine, or a flickering light at the end of the tunnel. We must continue to allow that light to be our encouragement.

Vision

For the light to inspire us, we must have a clear vision. Helen Keller said, "The only thing worse than being blind is a person that has his or her sight, but has no vision." Proverbs 29:19 reads, "Where there is no vision, the people perish."

When I talk to audiences, I like to pose positive questions: How many people are wealthy? How many people are in great health? How many people have spiritual abundance?

It is funny how quick people are to tell you how they have been and who they are if it is negative. They rarely mention positive things. I am not speaking of being arrogant or over confident. Just ask someone how they are doing and they will proceed to tell you. They will say things like, I am sick. I am poor. I am overweight. I am sad. I am depressed. I am unlucky. I am crazy, or I did something stupid the other day; you are not going to believe what I did. Automatically, your brain begins to compare your bad moments to theirs.

How many times have you asked someone how they have been and they have said, I have really been healthy for the past few days. SAY IT! I am rich! I have really been rich this week. I am intelligent! I did some intelligent things this month. Just pause for a minute and start to think of some of the smart things that you have done. If you are reading this book, you have done something smart :-).

Remember that idiot trying to pass you on the curve with two solid lines? He would never have had enough time to pass if you had not let him over. You slowed down, allowing him to pass, keeping him from killing himself and a bunch of other people. That was smart. How about the mistakes that your boss made, that you caught? Are you not glad you caught them, so it would not ruin his great reputation? Now you and all of your co-workers still have a job. What about the decision you made to not allow your child to go to that sleepover because you had a bad feeling. Later, you found out that a bunch of the kids were drunk, used drugs, went for a joy ride, and were arrested. You see, you have done some smart things.

You need to say to yourself, I am healthy, I am wealthy, I am smart, and I am spirit-filled. You will never become what you want to be by only speaking negatively. The mother of Isaiah Thomas, one of the NBA's fifty greatest players of all time, was asked about once being poor. She responded, "I've never been poor. I may have been broke, but I've never been poor. Being broke is temporary, but being poor is eternal." In essence, she redefined the term poor.

In elementary school, we used to play a game called IT. You could become IT just by being touched. The worst thing in the world was to be or have IT, especially if IT was the cooties. No one ever wanted to be IT or have IT. IT was not even real, but no one wanted IT. If you were ever touched, you did not run around saying that you were IT. That would have been a disgrace. The proper thing to do was to pass IT to someone else as quickly as you could. Either you denounced IT or you passed IT. Remember, you should never want to be IT. Do not ever be haunted by IT again. You are not IT and do not ever believe that you are IT again.

It may take you longer to understand, or you may learn differently than others, but you are not dumb. You may have some challenges with your health and you may not feel as good as you once did, but you are not sick. You may have not succeeded this time, but you are not a failure. Changing the labels that you place on your issues not only has a propensity to change the outcomes, but more importantly, it changes how you view and respond to those issues.

Drifters, Plodders, Clock-watchers, and Rut-makers

People who speak in the negative about their lives seem to act as victims. If you feel as though you are a victim, then you will not be motivated to take control of your life. Are you just drifting through life waiting for the day that they put you in a box? Do not wait on it, trust me, it will happen anyway. You might as well make your life as memorable of an experience as you can before you get there. Some people sit around and wait on life to happen to them instead of making things happen in life. I call these people drifters, plodders, rut-makers, and clock-watchers.

These people watch the clock for their morning and lunch breaks, and also for quitting time. They watch the clock to see when the meeting should have ended. They watch the clock to see what time dinner was supposed to start. They have specific bed times. They are only concerned with getting a little more sleep. They are always computing their sick and vacation times at work. They only keep up with the number of days they have left to call-in sick. They are like zombies. All of their days run together. You can hypnotize them and drop them off in the middle of next week and they will pick up where they left off because everyday is the same routine. They can operate their lives without missing a beat. They go to work the same way and see the same people. They consider being "in the zone" to be getting all the green lights on the way home. The only thing that they look forward to is forwarding the next joke to one hundred of their friends by email, sending a text message, logging on to their MySpace or Facebook accounts to do some social networking, gossiping about the day's current events, playing some computer or video games, twittering, watching or uploading their next video on YouTube, or making sure their cell phone has the coolest ringtone.

People who are really trying to create incredible lives for themselves always work a little longer than they should, do a little more than is expected, sleep a little less than the average, and put in more hours than what is required. You cannot expect to have an extraordinary life without putting in an extraordinary effort.

There has to be more to your life than merely existing. If you truly want to be more, you have to do more. You have to do the things that will keep you moving in the right direction. Yes, we all should have a little fun, play a little, and laugh some, but when your life is surrounded by and dependent upon unproductive activities, you cannot help but be unproductive.

Live Life with Passion

"Changing directions in life is not tragic; losing passion in life is."
                                                    -Max Lucado

When you are unproductive, it lessens your zeal and zest for life. When you do not have zeal and zest for life, it drags you down and others along with you. I do not like to hear people talk about what they hate or dislike, or how down on their luck they have been. They drop their shoulders, hold their heads down, and mope around as if someone has just stolen their lunch money.

When you are not living with passion, bad luck will find you. You will feel dismayed, troubled, and distressed. Passion must come from within. Imagine a one-hundred-meter sprinter not running with passion. Do you think he will win? Imagine what Simon Cowell would say to an American Idol contestant not singing with passion. She might as well walk off the stage before the comments start, to save herself the embarrassment. Try climbing Mt. Everest without passion. People often go into their businesses, occupations, and relationships without passion and then wonder why nothing exciting happens.

For some, the alarm clock snooze button was the best invention ever created. Because these people do not live their lives with passion, they are not excited to get out of bed and start a new day. They are not excited about the new challenges that life has to offer.

When we were in grade school, my parents had to threaten us with whippings to get us out of bed on regular school days, but on field trip days, we could hardly sleep. In fact, we would wake them up. You should live each day as if you are about to go on a field trip. Live each day as if it is going to be your last day on earth.

Dean Alfange said, "I do not choose to be a common man. It is my right to be uncommon. I seek opportunity to develop whatever talents God gave me -- not security. I do not wish to be a kept citizen, humbled and dulled by having the state look after me. I want to take the calculated risk; to dream and to build, to fail and to succeed... I prefer the challenges of life to the guaranteed existence; the thrill of fulfillment to the stale calm of utopia… I will never cower before any earthly master nor bend to any threat. It is my heritage to stand erect, proud, and unafraid; to think and act myself, enjoy the benefit of my creations and to face the world boldly and say—'This, with God's help, I have done'."

You may not be running around with a rag on your head, dressed in army fatigues, with an M-16 in your hands and a microphone on your lapel, broadcasting to everyone that you are Rambo when it comes to pursuing your goals. You may have a fire burning within. Henry David Thoreau said, "The mass of men lead lives of quiet desperation." We all have something inside of us that we want to let loose. We all have some contribution to make, some words to say, and gifts to give. The key is to not allow that desperation to remain quiet all of our lives.

Chapter 4: Are You Prepared?

"It's better to be prepared for an opportunity and not have one than to have an opportunity and not be prepared."

-Whitney M. Young, Jr.

A rabbi and a priest attend a boxing match. They watch as the boxers come into the ring. The rabbi sees one of the boxers as he motions the sign of the cross on himself. At that moment, the rabbi turns to the priest and says, "What does that mean?" The priest says, "Not a darn thing if the man can't fight."

You must be ready for your opportunity when it presents itself. People are sometimes so worried about getting an opportunity that they do not prepare for it. There are moments when you will not have time to make a game plan. If you are out of work, you may have to be prepared to start work today. Do not wait until you are called for an interview before you start shopping for a suit. Do not wait for a prospective employer to contact you and ask for a resume' before you start to work on it. Before your interview, you should have read everything you could about the company with which you are interviewing for. Be prepared for the opportunity before it comes.

There is nothing worse than the person who is always complaining about getting his shot, but when he gets his chance to shoot, he only shoots blanks. You have to work day and night preparing as if your opportunity will come tomorrow. If it does not, then at least you were prepared.

Move the Drill Down

You should not sit around and worry about misfortunes, but it is always a good idea to be prepared in case misfortunes should come your way. When I played college football, players were sometimes injured. It was considered part of the game. However, there was an efficient routine in place to deal with injuries when they occurred. First, the trainers would run out onto the field to work on the injured. Second, as he was receiving proper care, a coach would blow his whistle and yell, "Move the drill down ten yards." Lastly, the replacement player was coached to be ready in the event a player was deemed physically unable to continue. Coaches, players, trainers, and other staff members were always very concerned about the fallen family member and he always received top notch treatment. However, everyone also understood that it was part of the game and if we were going to have any chance at defeating our opponent, we had no choice but to move on without him.

Events that happen in life and business have to be viewed the same way. When problems arise in a company, production cannot stop. You do not have the luxury to worry about the order that fell through, or the business partner who quit. The company must continue to operate. The team must continue playing the game. It could be your business or your life in general. When something happens to parts of the team, those parts have to be replaced. Sometimes a missing person will be irreplaceable. Therefore, it may be practical to get two people to perform that job. If you have to start over, go ahead and do it now. Do not wait. If you wait, you will be gobbled up by the competition. Others will capitalize on your misfortunes quicker than you can blink. It has nothing to do with being cold or heartless. It is about picking up the broken pieces and moving on.

Setbacks

Picking up the broken pieces means that you do not allow setbacks to stop you. Just when you get things figured out, you have a setback. Setbacks throw people into a downward spiral. When you believe you are doing a good job of monitoring your weight, exercising regularly, eating healthy, drinking water, and staying away from fast food consistently for weeks, finding that you have gained five pounds could kill your diet. Maybe you are in business and you give what you feel is one of your best presentations ever, only to look around and see that no one seems to share your excitement. In these situations, you must stay on task. Many people give up hope during such setbacks. I contend that this is when you must fight harder than you ever have before.

My high school football coach, Scott Prichett (Coach Prig), used to tell us in practice that when bad things happened we should not feel sorry for ourselves. In your life, you can always find a hook of depression on which to hang your head. We can all reach into our history vaults of bad days and cry a little. We have all been treated as if we were worthless. Get over it. Pick yourself up and get on with getting on. Stop feeling sorry for yourself. You should refrain from making statements to yourself such as nobody loves me, God hates me, no one cares, and my mother must have left me on someone's doorstep. The harsh reality is that you will not be successful in anything you do in your life if you sit around and cry about the same old stuff.

So what if you have been abused - so have many others. The gas attendant is not going to award you twenty dollars worth of gas for your sorrows. So what if you have been mistreated - many people have. Stop calling up your friends and telling them the same story about why your husband left you. Let me be the one to tell you, in case you did not know, that your friends are tired of listening to that same old song. No one cares if you used to have a thriving business and now it is defunct. No one cares that you were doing well until you lost all of your money in the stock market. No one cares if you lost all of your life-long treasures in a fire ten years ago. No one is going to dwell on that but you. No one cares if you used to be fit and in shape, but after being diagnosed with some rare disease and having to take loads of medicine, you gained one hundred pounds in three months.

The truth and fact of the matter is that you need to get your lazy behind off the couch, stop eating ice cream and cake all day, stop taking depression and nerve pills, and stop watching the Lifetime channel in hopes that they will buy your story. I am sorry if this hurts. I guess you need a shoulder to cry on and someone with whom to cry. BOO HOO! There you go. Now, please get up and get over yourself.

I used to coach little league football. Even though I was a very physical football player and I still love the physical nature of the game, it is hard for me at times to watch it up close and personal. It seems so violent. I used to watch those I coached as they were trying to learn to play. Many of them did not understand the physical nature of the game and that the hitting sometimes really hurt. More often than not, I would see a guy peel himself off the ground wincing in pain, with tears coming down his face. I would always ask him discretely if he was okay. Ninety-five percent of the time he would nod that he was ready to continue playing. There were many times that I would see one of those tough little cookies wipe the tears from his eyes, get in his football position, and play the next play in pain. He was not going to allow his opponents, parents, coaches, and friends to see him defeated.

Sometimes this is what you will have to do. You may have been up all night, dealing with the prospect that your husband has decided to leave you. However, you may have to give the presentation of a lifetime that same morning. If you have to cry until the time you walk through those double doors, then go ahead. But as you walk through those doors, wipe your tears, and perform as you never have before. If you get a tear in your eye during the presentation, tell your audience that it is allergies, then wipe your tears and continue with your presentation. You do not have time to wallow in self-pity over your setback. You have a milestone to reach, a goal to accomplish, and a life to share.

Blues legend Ray Charles was fifteen years old and away studying music education in a special school for blind children, when he learned of his mother's death. He went into a deep depression for several months afterwards. The pain was so great that he was hardly able to function. One day, Ma Beck, a woman that used to take care of him, said to him, "You must go on, Ray! Stop feeling sorry for yourself, your mother wouldn't like to see you like that!" Of course, he did move past his setback and became one of the greatest entertainers of all time.

When my little brother passed a few years ago, it was a difficult time for my family and I, as I mentioned previously. However, the next day after making arrangements, my family and I were on our way home when we had to stop for gas. As we were leaving, a lady recognized my parents, which happens quite often, and asked them why they were in the area. They told her that their youngest son had just been killed in a car accident the day before and that they had been working on the details of funeral arrangements. I did not even hear this lady acknowledge or process news of his death before she started to rant about her own stupid life. She proceeded to thank them for the encouragement and prayers that they had given her sometime ago. She was middle-aged and had been told by doctors that she could not have kids; furthermore, she had been in a relationship that was on the brink of failure. She explained that after all of their prayers and encouragement, she was now engaged to be married and was expecting her first child. She was so excited. As I listened to her, I became enraged. I thought to myself, how could she be so insensitive to what we were going through? Luckily enough for her, I was not driving, because I would have run her over.

The truth is, my actions did not matter. She would have never felt what we were feeling. You should never expect people to match your sadness during your setbacks. Do not get mad because people do not feel the same way as you you do about your situation. You cannot make people care even if they should.

President Bill Clinton tried to relate to the public when he uttered, "I feel your pain." I do not think that many people bought that line. As a matter of fact, this statement has been the butt of many jokes for many comedians throughout the years.

You will be hurt repeatedly waiting on people to feel your pain. You may have just been diagnosed with cancer, which is a devastating occurrence. However, if you are in the drive-thru line behind someone who is about to go postal on the sixteen-year-old employee who forgot to put mayonnaise on his chicken sandwich, do not get mad at him because you think that he lacks perspective. It is not your job to anoint everyone with perspective. We all need near-death experiences at times to help us with perspective.

Waiting on others will set you back more than anything else. You can count on people and they will disappoint you. When I was dating my wife, I went to her house once to visit. Just as I arrived at her house, I ran out of gas. As I was trying to figure out how I was going to get gas in my car, I saw a young boy riding his bike in the neighborhood. I called to him and asked him for a favor. I explained to him that I had run out of gas and needed to get to the store to fill my gas can. He explained to me that he could help. I had about ten dollars in quarters in the trunk of my car. I told him that if he went to the store and filled up my gas can, then he could keep all that was left over. At that time, gas was only about $1.20 a gallon so he stood to make at least eight bucks for his efforts. He agreed to the deal. I handed him the money and the gas can. He explained that he had to go to his grandmother's house, tell her where he was going, and take a shower before he could perform the task. He said to me, "I'll be right back." After about an hour of waiting on him, I finally figured out that he was not coming back. The gas station was only a mile or so down the street, and even with all that he had to do, it should not have taken him an hour. I have not seen that little boy again since.

Sometimes we are waiting on people and they are not coming. People will tell you that you can count on them and they will not be there. They will give you their word and that is all that you will have because they will not show. They will R.S.V.P and still will not come. You will have to realize they are not coming. Then, just like me, you will have to start walking. If you meet them on the way, then oh well, but what you cannot afford to do is sit there and wait on something that will never come.

I have had many people promise me all sorts of things. I have had promises of positions with companies, cash rewards, business partnerships, stock options in companies, etc. Many of these people are people whom I have helped or who owe me favors. However, if I waited on them to give me the boost I needed to live my dreams, then I would never live them. You cannot afford to wait on anyone to come and rescue you from your position. They are not coming. So stop looking out your window for your wife to come back after she left you for your best friend. Stop sitting by the phone waiting for your business partner to call, the one who stole all the money out of the bank account. Stop sitting at home waiting on the mailman to bring you a check. You can sit on the bank of the river for the next twenty years waiting on your ship to come in. The harsh reality is that your ship may never come. Your ship has probably docked somewhere else.

You have to continue to walk towards your destination so that these setbacks will not depress you. That is not to say that you still will not have problems. There will be times when you have to simply start your mission, and worry about problems later. Not everything may go as planned.

Before the Space Shuttle launches, at times the countdown must either be delayed or rescheduled. It almost never goes as planned. The astronauts have to take tools with them because they usually always have to make repairs while in space. Even with all the rigorous testing and the hundreds of thousands of combined man-hours that go into a mission, things still go wrong. Your life will not be any different. You may have to take-off in your endeavor first and repair the broken pieces later. Invariably, something will go wrong that either you did not plan for, or that you did not expect. This is no time to quit. Like those who participate in the space mission, you have to repair the broken pieces and continue the mission.

Get up, forget the promises and the issues that you once had, pick up the broken pieces, and move on. Do not ever feel so sorry for yourself that you allow setbacks to hinder you from achieving whatever you want to achieve.

Goals

One way of picking up the broken pieces is to have clear, concise goals. Knowing your objectives will allow you to replace the broken pieces with similar parts that move you toward your goals. Thus, goal-setting is essential. A goal is nothing more than a predetermined outcome of where you want to be or what you want to possess within a specific time frame. Most people do not like to set goals because it requires a commitment and it seems elementary. Setting goals simply helps you to manifest what you want in life. Setting goals is like writing a grocery list for what you want out of life.

Helen Schmidt said, "It must be born in mind that the tragedy of life doesn't lie in not reaching your goal. The tragedy lies in having no goal to reach. It isn't a calamity to die with dreams unfulfilled, but it is a calamity to not dream. It is not a disgrace not to reach the stars, but it is a disgrace to not have stars to reach for. Not failure, but low aim is a sin."

How many times have you gone to the grocery store without having a grocery list, and managed to get everything you needed? If you are like me, the answer is never! You can have one thing on your mind when you go in the grocery store and then become so distracted by other events to the point that you forget the one thing that you needed. Why? Because you did not have what you needed written down. You will never remember until you are out of the store and on your way home. Because once you are driving, you do not have as many distractions as you did in that chaotic grocery store. Those chocolate chip cookies on aisle eleven are out of sight and so are the people, banners, buggies, greeters, disorderly kids, etc.

Life is just like a grocery store in that there is a lot to choose from, so you must first know what you want. You then have to stay on task; looking, searching, and asking for directions until you find it. Our days are so hectic with all we have to do with work, paying bills, taking care of our spouses, kids, homes, relatives, visitors, etc., that most of the time we do not take time to think about our goals. We simply forget what we are living and working for. But a simple, three-step process will help us to remember. First, you should write and review your goals before you start each day. Second, you should review those goals at midday to assess your progress. Third, you should review them before you go to bed to see how productive you were during the course of the day.

You must set short-term goals in an effort to reach the long-term goals that you have. You have to do something each day to attain those larger goals. If this process is completed each day, you will eventually complete your goals. You will not want to continue to look at the same uncompleted tasks day after day.

It is amazing to me that if you ask a person if they would like to become financially secure, they will respond affirmatively. However, if you ask if they have a plan or some written goals by which to obtain that security, about ninety-five percent of those people do not. It is no wonder that one percent of the population owns about half of the world's wealth.

Jack Welch, Chairman and CEO of General Electric (GE) between 1981 and 2001, was named "Manager of the Century" in 1999 by Time Magazine for making GE the largest and most valuable company in the world. His net worth is over $700 million. He said that he had set a goal to be Chairman and CEO of the company ten years before he assumed the position.

Set some goals. You never know where they might take you.

Never Give Up

"Most people give up just when they're about to achieve success. They quit on the one-yard line. They give up at the last minute of the game, one foot from a winning touchdown."

-Ross Perot

Once a goal is set, you should work toward it with undeniable desire. Donny Deutsch interviewed Donald Trump on the television show The Next Big Idea. When asked what advice he would offer those trying to create extraordinary lives, Trump said that the one thing he lives by is never, never, never giving up.

Quitting cannot be an option. Dr. Wayne Dwyer said, "Don't do all you can, but do whatever it takes to make it happen."

Many times, we give up and quit before we ever start. We render verdicts without ever hearing the entire case. In court, the judge always instructs the jury to weigh all of the evidence in the case before rendering a verdict. The defense and the prosecution always make each side of the story sound convincing. For this reason, you need to hear arguments on both sides before judgments and opinions are made. Our lives are not any different. We often times only hear the story of why something will not work or why our situation is hopeless. We never take the time to weigh the possibilities of favorable outcomes.

Ed Love, late sculptor and Florida State University professor, used to get very angry when students would talk negatively about their futures. He would say, " If you know so much about next week then predict the lottery numbers." He would contend that if a person couldn't predict the lottery numbers then he or she couldn't tell him anything about next week. He would teach his students that just because things look grim today, that it does not mean that those situations will remain the same tomorrow.

Winston Churchill said, "We must learn to be equally good at what is short and sharp and what is long and tough. You cannot tell from appearances how things will go." He went on to say, "Never give in, never, never, never, never - in nothing great or small, large or petty - never give in except to convictions of honor and good sense. Never yield to force; never yield to the apparently overwhelming might of the enemy. We have only to persevere to conquer."

Jimmy Valvano had one of the greatest Cinderella victories in the history of the NCAA tournament when he coached North Carolina State to a national championship victory over giants, the Houston Cougars, featuring future pro basketball Hall of Famers Hakeem "The Dream" Olajawon and Clyde "The Glyde" Drexler. He was later stricken with cancer.

He became even more popular for his battle against cancer and fundraising efforts for cancer research. He made one of his most memorable speeches during the Excellence in Sports Performance Yearly (ESPY) awards. The speech is repeatedly aired. In his speech, he spoke about how precious the time he had left was. He explained there are three things that we should all do each day: laugh, think, and be moved to tears through happiness and joy. He believed that these things would make for full and special days. He later went on to say that you should keep your dreams alive in spite of problems or issues you may have. He explained that he wanted to spend whatever time he had left giving hope to others. Finally he said, "Cancer can take away all my physical abilities, but it cannot touch my mind, it cannot touch my heart, and it cannot touch my soul. Those three things are going to carry on forever."

He shows that in the face of everything - keep fighting. Keep hoping. Keep dreaming. In the spirit of it all, never give in. In the hope of triumph - try, try, try, and try again. This is the only way victory will be attained. Your attitude should match his foundation's motto: Don't give up, don't ever give up.

Conquering Fear

"We know deeply that the other side of every fear is a freedom."
-Marilyn Ferguson

Many people give up because they are afraid. Many people do not act because of this crippling emotion. Others do not even start because of fear. Fear is the emotion that causes people to fail more than all of the other emotions combined. You cannot be afraid to try. Nothing can be accomplished without an attempt. Getting rid of the fear in your life is one of the most important steps that you can undertake. Living in fear invariably keeps you from being productive. When fear arises you need to push it out and away from your life.

I used to be very afraid of everything: the dark, approaching people, taking on challenges, failure, rejection, and success. I am inclined to believe that everyone throughout their day, encounters some sort of fear. You are only born with two fears: the fears of loud sounds and of falling. All other fears are learned. There are two ways that these fears are learned. The first way is from your own experiences. The second way is from the experiences of others. Fear should be a cause for success rather than an excuse for failure.

What you must do is learn how to channel your fear. A number of famous athletes and entertainers say that they become very nervous before performing. Magic Johnson stated that he was very nervous when he had to play center in the NBA finals during his rookie season in place of Kareem Abdul Jabbarr. He poured in forty-two points, grabbed fifteen rebounds, dished out seven assists, and had three steals to help his team win the NBA championship. He was voted the finals MVP. Before he won his third NBA championship, Tim Duncan has said that he was as nervous as he had ever been. Michael Douglas has said that he used to vomit before all of his stage performances. Hall of Fame quarterback Fran Tarkenton has said that when you stop feeling butterflies, it is time to get out of the game. Elvis, after nearly twenty years of performing, stated that he still became nervous before going onstage.

The key is to not allow nervousness to turn into fear and paralyze you. Many people freeze up in the clutch, but the greats use that fear to allow their talent to flow. I have given many speeches in my life. Although I may have looked and sounded comfortable prior to giving those speeches, in most cases, I was so nervous that I could hardly breathe.

Michael Phelps, Olympic swimming gold medalist, once said, "You've got to set goals before you try to do anything. When you get nervous or anxious, take small steps to try and reach the bigger goals."

Rejection

One of the biggest fears that people have is that they will fail, and ultimately, be rejected. Bonaro W. Overstreet said, "Perhaps the most important thing we can undertake toward the reduction of fear is to make it easier for people to accept themselves, to like themselves."

We have all felt rejected at one time or another. When you were younger, maybe you did not fit in. Maybe your father was not around. Maybe you were not chosen for the cheerleading squad, football team, or school play. Maybe you thought that your mother liked your sister more. Whatever happened, you felt rejected. For some, that makes them work even harder. For others, it makes them give up and never try again. The rejection is too overwhelming for them. For Michael Jordan, being cut from the varsity basketball team during his freshman year made him practice and work on his game, and it did not hurt that he grew about six inches over the next summer.

Dorothy Thompson said, "Once you understand that rejection is just a part of the process to attainment as acceptance, then it doesn't hurt as bad and it doesn't mean as much to you to be rejected… only when we are no longer afraid do we begin to live." Some of us will do anything to avoid rejection. Sometimes that means not even trying. I have spoken to many who were afraid to engage in business; they were afraid of rejection. Most successful businessmen, on average, had started fifteen businesses before they became successful. They were not afraid of a little rejection, a few no's, or people thinking that they were deranged.

What will you do in the face of rejection? Will you fold the tent up and go home like everyone else? Or will you roll up your sleeves and get to work? Remember, you only have to be right once. You only have to pick the right business once or find one good prospect. You only have to have one great idea. You can meet the right producer, director, or agent, and your life could change overnight. You could be all wrong up until that point. Bo Bennett said, "Rejection is nothing more than a necessary step in the pursuit of success."

We all want people to like us and think that we are successful people. All the great accomplishments had failures first. Thomas Edison failed some 17,000 times at inventing the light bulb. The Wright brothers failed miserably on numerous occasions before they took flight. A Hall of Fame baseball player only hits the ball about three out of every ten times at bat. However, you cannot go to the plate hoping not to strike out. No player has made it to the Hall of Fame based only on how many times he walked. You have to swing at some point. Babe Ruth was one of the greatest baseball players and home-run hitters ever, but he also struck out more times than anyone else.

What if you sold a product to three out of every ten people? What if three out of every ten people signed on as a distributor in your organization? In most cases, your ratios do not have to be that high to garner success. We put too much pressure on ourselves to perform at every level and in every situation. When one, two, or three people reject us, we feel like everyone else will also. Remember, if the right person sees your vision, he or she will bolt you to the top quicker than hundreds of rejections. Discontinue worrying about getting everyone to jump onboard. Stop worrying about being rejected. If you go through your whole life without any failures, then you will look at your life as a failure because it would mean that you never tried anything.

Coach Prig believed that you should try to carry out your assignments correctly. He believed that if you make a mistake then you should make that mistake at full speed.

You have to be willing to acknowledge your faults and move on. No one has lived a mistake-free life. Once you admit your mistakes, you will feel better about yourself and others will respect you.

Whatever you are losing sleep over, in whatever professional, business, or personal situation you are in, you must not take your focus away from the big picture. Yes, these are big decisions that can make or break a career, but you have to take the risk.

In early contractual obligations, you sometimes have to give up more than you anticipated. As long as you are not selling your soul, you have to choose and move. Many people are so attached to finding the best deal that they never act. I have cried when I felt I did not get the best deal. The product will always go on sale the day after you buy it. I have been in the grocery store and thought myself an idiot for not choosing the fastest checkout line. It has nothing to do with doing your due diligence before you spend your hard-earned money, start your business, or choose your web-hosting company. You cannot allow finding the best deal to cripple you and keep you from acting.

I am embarrassed to say that it took me over two years to get a simple web site to promote my personal development and speaking company. I could not decide on a web-hosting company, domain name, or type of web site. This is ridiculous when there are companies that have systems in place whereby a person can have a web site with a unique domain name up and running within a few hours. I was haggling over two and three dollars per month or some feature that one company had versus another.

If you are an inventor, you eventually have to choose an avenue to get your product to market. You cannot stay stuck forever on getting the cheapest manufacturer for your product If you are a writer, you cannot struggle with the layout for your book cover for a year. Making decisions is a process. I have known people who cannot find a church and have been looking for five and ten years. Moreover, there are people who cannot find a church worthy to receive ten percent of their earnings because they think that all church officials are unethical.

Some things are out of your control. If you are in a band, you do not have time to audition a new bass player for two years after the current bass player quits. If you are a record company, you cannot spend so much time tweaking the title song for your artist's album that it never debuts. You cannot push the release date back forever. Someone bigger and better will always release his or her album at the same time. At some point, the title song has to be chosen and a release date set. You may be a race-car driver struggling with choosing a crew chief. Pick one and live with your decision. Whatever decision you make, just know that you made the best decision possible at the time with the information available. Do not be afraid to make a decision and live with it.

> *There was a very cautious man*
> *Who never laughed or prayed;*
> *He never sang, he never cried,*
> *He never risked, and he never tried.*
> *Then one day he passed away,*
> *His insurance was denied;*
> *Since he never really lived,*
> *They claimed he never really died.*
> *- Author Unknown*

Look Out For Yourself

Numerous times, I have made decisions in an attempt to please others. I hesitated because of what I thought others would think of me. In most of these cases, I received the short end of the stick. You should always, and I mean always, look out for yourself. It may sound selfish, but it is very true. You are the only person who will look out for you. Do not allow people to step on you all of your life.

If you have a product to sell, you should sell it at its value. It is not ungodly to build a profit into your product or service. Do you think that Bill Gates, since becoming the richest man in the world, is going to start giving away his software? I do not think so. It is what it is. You do not have to step on others to get what you want, but I do think that you have to step over them. It is always the second rat who gets the cheese. The first rat gets caught in the trap. The second rat gets his stomach full. You cannot help everyone. You cannot help others until you help yourself. Therefore, your conscience has to be strengthened and your skin thickened.

You must remember Harriet Tubman was off the plantation when she went back to help others. She used the Underground Railroad, which was a secret path used by the slaves, to help them make it safely to freedom. However, she shot those who tried to turn back because they would have put her life and the lives of others in jeopardy. She knew that they would have succumbed to the pressure and given up the secrets of the Underground Railroad to slave masters. In essence, she had to look out for herself and those that wanted help.

You cannot have family members and friends that you love so much that they send you back to the plantation. You cannot give away all that you have worked for to people who are lazy, shiftless and will never do anything with their lives. Rapper MC Hammer made roughly forty million dollars in one of his best years as an entertainer. However, he ended up losing his fortune. First, there was a lot of mismanaging of his assets. Second, he tried to help everyone from his old neighborhood by practically giving away all of his money. He had an estimated 800 person staff that he was paying weekly during the height of his success. These people were not doing anything but standing on and around the stage while he performed.

Oprah said that one of the first things she had to learn to do after she became successful was say no.

Comedian, Radio Personality, and Best –Selling Author Steve Harvey said that one of the best pieces of advice that he ever received was that the best way to help the poor is not to be one of them.

Bill Walton, speaking about LeBron James coming into the NBA and receiving a 100 million-dollar endorsement deal from NIKE alone, said that the one thing that he must realize, that the great John Wooden taught, is to never do anything for people that they could normally do for themselves. Help people, but understand that you cannot save the world.

Mentors

"No one lives long enough or is smart enough to learn everything they need to learn starting from scratch. To be successful, we absolutely, positively have to find people who have already blazed a trail for us to follow."

-Brian Tracy

I believe that you not only have to surround yourself with good people in order to get the success you want, but also to maintain it. The one thing that is worse than not having success is having success and losing it. Good mentors can help you in both areas. They teach you how to stay level headed and grounded through any situation that you may encounter. I call these people General Mentors and Specialized Mentors.

General Mentors

General Mentors are people who have wisdom and are willing to share it. They have a broad range of knowledge. They are very wise. They are the people that you can consult with about any situation that you face. He or she could be a friend, teacher, coach, colleague, parent, or pastor.

They are people who are honest with you and pull no punches. They are trustworthy and respected. You do not have to worry about them taking your business to the evening news. They have your best interests at heart. They never have any personal agendas. General Mentors practice what they preach. They are honest whether it hurts or not. They teach you how to handle success and failure. They are always cool, calm, and collected. They are positive and full of encouragement.

My parents are my General Mentors. They have always been able to give me direction. If I had to make decisions that would cost me money or time, or decisions that would only add to my problems, I could always count on them to steer me in the right direction. They have been mentors to countless others also. They are role models in every sense of the word.

Many people do not have mentors, or they had them at some point but they are gone now. Thus, they end up reflecting on advice or words from times past. Some people do not have family members or friends they can trust; so they have to look to others to be their General Mentors. They have to read inspirational books, counsel with their pastors, and hire life coaches.

General Mentors have the experience and the expertise to attack problems. If they do not know the answer, they can get you to people who do. They are very resourceful. A General Mentor is always someone on the outside looking in. If they are not totally on the outside, they can take themselves outside and look at each problem objectively. You will find that General Mentors are very important to your success.

Specialized Mentors

Specialized Mentors are mentors in your field of endeavor. This person may not be a friend or someone you know. You may even have to pay a huge sum for his or her knowledge. He or she should be successful in that particular field. Some doctors are general practitioners and some are medical specialists. When the general practitioner orders an EKG and believes that you may have a problem with your heart, he or she refers you to a cardiologist. If you have an issue with your brain, he or she sends you to a neurologist. These doctors are specialists in these particular areas.

Your specialized mentor should be able to guide you through the maze and help you reduce the learning curve. He or she should be proven in the field and be a good teacher. Not everyone who knows something can teach it to someone else. Therefore, you should find someone who knows and can teach.

Be careful not to confuse a person's success with sheer luck. Do not ask the lottery winner to be your stockbroker the day after he wins the lottery. If you want a successful website, find a person whose site ranks at or near the top of search engines. Inventors know the process of finding an engineer for your product and how to get it to market fast. There are coaching consultants that can assist you in teaching teamwork to your team. There are others who are able to help you in the start up phase of your advertising company. There are great mentors who are experienced at prospecting, contacting and inviting, and giving presentations, who are able to teach you proven time tested techniques to use in your multi level/network marketing business. Brig Hart, who is considered one of the top network marketing experts in the country, teaches that the S.Y.S.T.E.M. is the most important component of any network marketing organization. He says that it is an acronym for Save Yourself Time Energy and Money. He further states that a huge part of the SYSTEM is not reinventing the wheel, but doing those things that have been tested and shown to work time and time again by people who are already successful.

You may have to find more than one mentor. That is perfectly fine as long as you get the help and the advice that you need to succeed. The best, brightest, and most successful people in the world have all had and still have mentors. The smartest thing that you can do is to get advice from someone who has experience. Some people are too proud to ask for advice. That is almost a sure way to fail. Find mentors in your life; they will help you succeed.

Chapter 5: You Are Weird

"Doubt is to certainty as neurosis is to psychosis. The neurotic is in doubt and has fears about persons and things; the psychotic has convictions and makes claims about them. In short, the neurotic has problems, the psychotic has solutions."

-Thomas Szasz

Are you a person that marches to the beat of a different drummer? Do people look at you sometimes and shake their head? Are people shooting you and your ideas down? Do people stop talking when you walk into the room? If you answered yes to any of these questions, then you are probably on the right track to success. Henry Ford, by many accounts, was considered an ignoramus. Someone once asked him how many feet are in a mile. He explained that he did not know, but he could find someone who did in less than five minutes.

Will Smith, who went from small to big time as a rapper/singer/entertainer and one of Hollywood's leading men, said that the key to his success was "psychotic drive."

A little girl from Houston, Texas was characterized by her friends as dancing so hard that it looked like she was having convulsions. Her name was Beyonce Knowles. Before embarking on her very successful solo career, she was formerly the lead singer of Destiny's Child, who, according to the World Wide Music Awards, is the best selling female group of all time.

If people look at you as being a little weird, somewhat over the top, someone whose screws are a little loose, then you should think to yourself that you are probably on the right track. You may not be marching to any beat, but rather skipping to a tune.

Remember King David was not his father's first choice as the son he thought would be anointed King. David was always singing, talking to himself, and bothering with those sheep. So go ahead, be maniacal, a little psychotic, crazy, and somewhat weird. All of that is fine. When you are looking down from the mountain top of success, then you can scream and ask—who is crazy now?

In the movie, Dead Poets Society, John Keating (Robin Williams) uses a Latin phrase with his students: Carpe Diem. It means, "Seize the Day." It is a reminder for them to not take life for granted and to live each day of their lives to the fullest, getting the most out of each day. What if you tried to get the most out of each and every day? Ask yourself what you would do if you knew you could not fail. Where would you go? What would you try? Whom would you call? I contend that there will be many people in heaven looking back at their lives realizing that they should have taken more chances and tried a little harder. God is going to show us that everything we ever wanted was there for the taking; all we had to do was ask questions or try an idea.

Michael Phelps, after winning six gold and two bronze medals in the 2004 Summer Olympics, and later eight at the 2008 Olympic Games, was asked about his thought process before competing. He said that he was thinking that he may only have one chance and that he needed to take advantage of his opportunity. Once opportunities are lost, they may never come again. Opportunities are not lost; they just go to someone else. James Dean said, "Dream as if you'll live forever and live as though you'll die today."

I have often heard that you should pray as if it all depends on God and work like it all depends on you. People live their whole lives as if they will have a million opportunities. It is always the people who do not maximize their potential in their areas of interest who have the most regrets. You can go in most neighborhoods and the locals will talk of the playground legends and tell stories of how the best athletes never even got out of the city. They did not seize the opportunity that they had. It is always the person that has done the least for their loved one who has passed, who puts on the biggest show at the funeral. It is up to you to take advantage of the opportunities that you have. Do not take anyone or anything for granted because it or they may not be there tomorrow. Remember to always be grateful for what you have and to give thanks for where you are. Try to live in the moment as much as you can because once it is gone, it is gone forever.

The Youth and Youthful Thinking

Children always seem to live in the moment. Children, like Trevor in the movie Pay It Forward, do what I call, believe hard. They believe that they can change the world. Their faith is unmatched. If you ask a child what he or she wants to be, he or she will often say a doctor, lawyer, police officer, teacher, cheerleader, football player, or basketball player, and, oh yes, a scientist, astronaut, or biologist. They say it without wavering. As we get older, we start to think that maybe we cannot. By the time people are in their early to mid-thirties, they do not believe that they can do anything. By the time they are in their fifties and sixties, the word "belief" has all but evaporated from their vocabulary. To be successful, you must believe like a child no matter how old you are. You will not be successful unless you can blot out the negative and say, yes, I can make this work. Yes, there is a market for this product. Someone may have thought of this, but my idea is unique for several reasons.

Youngsters, living in the moment with this believe-hard attitude, have brought forth some of the greatest ideas, developments, and inventions ever created. Bill Gates was twenty years old when he started Microsoft. Michael Dell was nineteen years old when he dropped out of college to run Dell Computers, Inc. At thirty-two, William King invented the world's smallest soldering iron. At thirty-three, Matthew Brand's research led to the creation of "digital puppets," a company that incorporates not just the appearance, but also the mannerisms of movie stars. Sky Dayton was twenty-three years old when he founded EarthLink Network, now one of the nation's top five internet service providers. Mark Zuckerberg was nineteen years old when he founded Facebook. Larry Page and Sergey Brin were twenty-five years old when they started Google, and today, they have a net worth of $16.6 billion, each. Chad Hurley, twenty-eight, Steve Chin, twenty-seven, and Jawed Karim, twenty-six, founded YouTube, which they sold to Google, earning $326 million, $326 million, and $64 million, respectively.

This youthful, believe-hard thinking is not aimed at the young in chronological age, but to the young in spirit. I do not think of a person as being old. I just think of them as having experience. However, even if you think of yourself as being old, you should keep your youthful, living-in-the-moment attitude. You have to believe that what you are working on will work. The problem is that when we get older, we start to think that all possible ideas have been spent. We start to think that there is no need to try. People really start to think that they are too old when they start to look around them or back in time. Age should not mean that your life is over. It could be the beginning. The Chinese bamboo tree has to be watered and nurtured for five years before it grows over ninety feet in six weeks. You are not too old unless you think you are. Maybe you have been in your watering process for all of this time. Here are some people of age who continued to **believe hard**:

Poet Robert Frost was forty-eight when he wrote his most frequently reprinted work, "Stopping by the Woods on a Snowy Evening."

Colonel Sanders was sixty-two when he founded Kentucky Fried Chicken. That is youthful thinking.

Mr. W. K. Kellogg was forty-six when he started his Kellogg cereal business.

Ralph Ellison was forty-one when he published Invisible Man.

Danny Trejo, a famous actor, was well into his forties when he began his ascent in Hollywood.

Famed football coach Vince Lombardi was in his late forties when he started his successful football run.

Winston Churchill became Prime Minister of England at age sixty-two.

Walt Disney was fifty-three when he opened Disneyland. He was sixty-five when he began work to open Disney World.

A person's age is in direct correlation to his or her spirit. There are certain things that zap people's spirit, habits they can control like the use of cigarettes, drugs, and alcohol. You should refrain from these habits. Doing so will help you to not only keep your spirit, but also help you to look and feel younger. Have you ever looked at someone and thought, my goodness she looks bad. She appears twenty years older than she is because of the lifestyle that she is living. How you think you look dictates how you feel about yourself. Helen Keller said, "One should never count the years, one should instead count one's interests. I have kept young trying never to lose my childhood sense of wonderment. I am glad I still have a vivid curiosity about the world I live."

When you have some experience under your belt, you should keep your youthful thoughts. If you are here, it is for a reason. You should not believe that you are here to just exist. You must believe that you still have contributions to make. You still have a message, a story, and a life to share. Do not allow any obstacle to stand in your way. You still have some mountains to conquer and some dreams to make come true.

Remembering Your Past Victories

Whether you are young, old, or in between, you are already prepared with everything you need to defeat the obstacles that you are facing in your life. You were made for this day. God does not give you a dream without giving you the ability to make that dream come true. Dr. Joyce Brothers said, "Success is a state of mind. If you want success, start thinking of yourself as a success."

We all have been victorious at some point in our lives. The problem is that we forget those victories and only remember the failures. Before David went to fight Goliath, Saul doubted David's ability. He noted that Goliath had been a warrior for many years and that David himself was young and inexperienced. David did not fall into this doubtful thinking. He reminded Saul what he had done to the lion that took one of the sheep out of the flock he had been watching. He explained to Saul that he had taken the sheep out of the lion's mouth, grabbed him by his beard, and killed him. He told Saul that he had killed a bear also. He explained that Goliath would be no different. David remembered his past victories. He did not sit and think about the times when he did not manage the flock well or had misplayed his harp.

Before you go to fight your Goliath, you need to recall your past victories. In fact, you need to write down all the successes that you have had in your life. They do not have to be special to everyone, only special to you. A victory for you could have been purchasing a vehicle at your negotiated price or being able to buy a home. You could have finally gotten the nerve to ask your boss for a raise. Maybe you went back to college and received that degree you had desired for years. Your victory could have been acquiring a trade or completing some home improvement projects. It could have been figuring out how to work a computer program.

Write your victories down. Look at them every day. When you are facing a daunting challenge, you should recall them. Then, you will be better equipped to fight those Goliaths in your life. Your past victories will help you gain the confidence that is needed to be successful.

Stories of Triumph

Every successful person has had to defeat Goliaths and obstacles in their lives before they became successful. Thus, you will have to do the same.

One such lady worked as a reporter for a newspaper and later had to quit her job because of arthritis in her ankles and feet. She was mostly bedridden and lived in what she called a "dump." Her husband would bring her books to read until one day he grew tired of bringing her books, and he told her that she should write one herself. When she asked what she should write about, he told her to write about something with which she was familiar. She finally wrote her book. She tried and failed thirty-three times before someone decided to publish it. It would later land her the Pulitzer Prize. She would later write,

"If the novel has a theme it is that of survival. What makes some people able to come through catastrophes, while others are apparently just as able, strong, and brave, go under? It happens in every upheaval. Some people survive; others don't. What qualities are in those who fight their way through triumphantly that are lacking in those who go under....? I only know that the survivors used to call that quality gumption. So I wrote about the people who had gumption and the people who didn't."

Her name was Margaret Mitchell and the title of her book was *Gone with the Wind*.

Three young girls were trying desperately to get their music heard. They were nicknamed "The No Hits" because of their many unsuccessful attempts. They had six songs that failed; then they recorded a little song titled, *Where Did Our Love Go?* It was their first single to go #1. They were The Supremes.

What about the fellow who left his small town in Georgia and traveled to San Francisco in pursuit of his dream. While living in a boat house and occasionally sitting out on a dock he would watch the boats leave and come again. He seemingly contemplated giving up on his dream of becoming a successful singer/songwriter. He would later record his thoughts in song. The singer was Otis Redding and the song, which became a #1 hit single, was of course, Sittin' on the Dock of the Bay

James Earl Jones was a stutterer as a young student actor. On numerous occasions, he had to write notes to his friends to communicate. He is now known as one of the greatest communicators and orators of our time.

Dave Thomas was adopted. He lost his mother when he was five. His father married three more times after his adoptive mother's death. His family was constantly moving around. He was a high school dropout who worked in and managed a few KFC restaurants before deciding to start his own fast food restaurant. He named his restaurant Wendy's.

Elvis Presley was shy, picked on as a child, and stuttered. After one of his early performances on the Milton Berle show, the New York Times said, "He has no discernible talent." He's now known simply as, "The King."

Eddie Arcaro rode over 250 loses before he became a winner. He ended his career with over 4,779 wins. He had five derby wins, $30,039,543 in purses, a record six Preakness' and six Belmonts' and was one of only two jockeys to win the Kentucky Derby five times. He was the only jockey to win the Triple Crown (the Kentucky Derby, the Preakness, and the Belmont Stakes) twice.

Walt Disney's first submission of drawings for publication was not successful. In fact, he was told that he had no artistic talent. His vision only gave us the world of Disney, which includes all the characters, theme parks, television stations, and a Hollywood studio.

Wilma Rudolph was born prematurely and later developed double pneumonia twice, as well as scarlet fever. She was later stricken with polio and her leg was left crooked and her foot turned inward. She could barely walk to do anything at times, and the pain seemed to be endless. She spent most of her childhood in braces. She grew increasingly tired of walking around in those braces. She began to take those braces off and walk without them. She later proved to everyone that she did not need those braces any longer. At age thirteen, she started to play sports. She played basketball, ran track, and later joined the Tennessee State University Tigerbelles. She became the first African American woman to win three gold medals in track and field at the Olympic Games.

Charlie Chaplin once lost his own look-a-like contest. He did not even make the finals.

During an audition, there was a young man who was told he had no acting talent, could not sing, and could only dance a little bit. His name was Fred Astaire.

Lauryn Hill was once booed while performing at the Apollo Theater; she later went on to win eight Grammys.

Julia Roberts was the fourth choice for the role she played in Pretty Woman.

These stories illustrate the message that defeating those Goliaths in your life is necessary. Getting through those barriers requires unshakable courage and commitment. Everyone has had to get through them and so will you. So prepare yourself, move past those obstacles. Do as David did and cut the head off those Goliaths so they will never spring up again.

Chapter 6: The Hunter and the Bird

Sometimes we stare so long at the door that is closing that we see too late the one that is open.

— **Alexander Graham Bell**

The Hunter and the Bird

A hunter went to Africa in hopes of getting a huge kill. While he was there looking for the next biggest kill, he came across some exotic birds. He saw one that he really liked so he flipped out his net, caught the bird, put him in a cage, and carried him home. The hunter kept the bird for years, feeding him well, giving him a nice cage to live in, and treating him with a great deal of respect. He later discovered that the bird could talk. The hunter created a bond with him. After many years passed, the hunter decided to go on another big hunt to Africa. He asked the bird if there were any messages that he wanted to relay to his friends. He said, "Yes, by the way I do. I want you to tell all my friends that I'm happy, I love my new home, my cage has everything in it that I ever dreamed of, and my owner has given me the chance to experience a high quality life."

So the hunter went back to Africa, found the friends of the bird, and delivered the message. He told them that their friend was fine, loved his new home, and that he had a quality of life that was unmatched. Just as he said that, one of the birds fell to the ground, legs in the air, eyes wide open, and stiff as a board. The hunter thought to himself that the message of his friend doing well must have shocked him enough to kill him. After arriving home, he told his pet bird about his trip. The bird asked him if he had indeed found his friends and the hunter said, "Yes." The bird anxious to hear how they were doing asked frantically what they had to say and if there were any messages. The hunter told him that they all were fine except for one of them. He said,

"Funny thing happened when I told them how great you were doing here with me and how good of friends we had become. I explained to them that I often have you sing and show you off to my friends, and that everyone thinks that you were a wonderful catch. Just as I finished telling your friends the good news one of them fell to the ground, legs in the air, eyes wide open, stiff as a board." The bird said, "Well that's awful." "Yeah," said the hunter, "for him to just die like that from hearing the good news."

So the next morning, the hunter awoke as usual and went to speak to the bird. However, when he looked in the cage, he saw that his pet was in his cage, stiff as a board. The hunter was sad. He reached in the cage carefully, took him out, and laid him on the ground on a towel. He began digging him a grave. As he was finishing the burial preparation, the hunter turned to pick him up and noticed that he was gone. He looked up in the tree and there his pet was just as well as ever. The hunter said, "You tricked me. That was a cruel trick to play. I thought that you had died from the story that I told of your friend passing." The bird said, "No, what happened was when you went to Africa and told them my story, they knew that I wasn't happy and I wanted to be free. My friend, who you thought had died from my message, was really sending me a message. He was telling me that before I could live again, I first had to die."

In St. John 3:3, Jesus tells Nicodemus that, "Except a man is born again he cannot see the Kingdom of God." In I Corinthians 15:31, Paul writes, "I die daily."

To be a new person and create the life that you want for yourself, you must first die. This is not a physical death. You must give up some of the habits and ideologies of the past. You must not allow the same issues and problems that have caused you to be in your current state to keep you there. You cannot continue to harbor those same old stale outdated ideas. Before you can move on to a better position in life, you have to die first. You have to kill that old person that has been hindering you. You must rid yourself of the old person who used to procrastinate. The person who used to allow fear to control him must be gone. You must become someone new. You must put the past behind you.

Hall of Fame sports broadcaster Dick Vitale says that the two most wasted days of the year are tomorrow and yesterday. People are always talking about the past. They allow the past to dictate their future. Your past does not equal your future. Just because yesterday was a bad day does not mean tomorrow will be the same. Just because you failed last week, does not mean that you have to fail this week.

Joel Osteen says, "People respond when you tell them 'there is a great future in front of you, you can leave your past behind.'"

Stop looking at yesterday. When you look at yesterday in a negative way, what you see is: YES-TERD-AY. So let it go! It is over! It is in the past, so move on. Do not wallow in yesterday. If you wallow in yesterday, you will reek of sadness, disdain, contempt, neglect, and scorn.

Some people are trapped inside of a body and mind that they hate because they are the same as they were five, ten, or twenty years ago. They are still holding on to theories that are no longer valid. They still believe that they do not deserve to have healthy relationships. They believe that they have to be abused to be loved. They believe that average is good. They think that the good side of life is only for others.

Most people try to suppress issues in their lives. They try to hide the problems that they have had. When you hide them then they become like the jack in the box. As you turn the handle that old person gets closer and closer to popping out. And one day, BAM! You cannot just hide those issues; they must be gone. They must be buried. Get rid of that old person so you do not have to see him or her again.

Bigger and Better

"A competitor will find a way to win. Competitors take bad breaks and use them to drive themselves just that much harder. Quitters take bad breaks and use them as reasons to give up. It's all a matter of pride."

-Nancy Lopez

If you start to think about what happened in the past, then you will never believe that you can go to new heights. However, if you look past the past, you will find that often times you will be able to perform greater feats than you ever did before.

The Hunter and the Bird

In one of Michael Jordan's final slam-dunk competitions, it came down to an epic battle between him and Dominique Wilkins. They were both performing unbelievable dunks. Michael Jordan performed one of his "walk the sky, rock the baby, single-handed throw down" dunks. Dominique Wilkins was shown on the sideline in respectful disbelief. He applauded Michael's performance. Then he said, "Now I've got to come up with something nastier." In essence he was saying that he had to create a better dunk than Michael's to win. Dominique ended up performing one of the best dunks he ever displayed in a slam-dunk competition.

If you are in business and your competitor comes out with a great product, you should applaud them for being innovative, go back to the drawing board, and come up with something bigger and better. As Dominique thought, you have to elevate your game. Take it too new heights. You should never give in and think that the fight is over. When someone comes out with a hit song, as a singer, songwriter, or producer you should get back in the studio and come up with an even better song and arrangement. This will ultimately make you better. Do not just sit there with a defeatist attitude. Moping will not get you anywhere. Do not sit around building up negative emotions about the competition. Make it your business to make them talk about you.

It happens all the time in NASCAR. You will see a team consistently start to win. It appears that they are a step ahead of all of the other teams. They have found new technology that makes their car run faster, more efficiently, and better than every other car in the field. The other teams now have to spend more hours in the garage coming up with better strategies and solutions to remain competitive.

It happens in the area of technology too. Google, for instance, introduced its mapping software called Google Earth. Microsoft, trying not to be outdone, introduced 3D Virtual Earth.

Competition should bring out the best in you. You do not get better by being jealous. Figure skater Tonya Harding lost her entire career when it was discovered that she was involved in a plot that left her fellow competitor Nancy Kerrigan maimed. Harding could not deal with the prospect of having Kerrigan as a competitor in the World Championships, so she and her ex-husband paid someone to break Kerrigan's legs. Even though Harding won the championship, she was later stripped of her title.

You do not have to cheat, beat up your opponent, or resort to unethical schemes to win. Do what it takes to win, but do it within the confines of the rules while maintaining integrity, class, and dignity.

Improve, but Keep Your Originality

While you are getting better, you must understand that you are an original. Giving up that which makes you who you are is not always the best solution. You have to learn how to kill the worst parts of you, while keeping alive the best parts.

In the mid-1980s, Pepsi conducted taste tests around the country. They had people blindly taste their product and Coca-Cola to see which customers preferred. Pepsi won the challenge because they started to use more vanillin than vanilla. During a taste test, customers chose the sweeter taste. Later, Coca-Cola introduced New Coke and it beat out both the regular Coke and Pepsi in taste tests. In order to introduce New Coke to the market, executives launched a campaign. It was a huge business and commercial failure. People hated it. Their sales plummeted. Within a couple of months, they returned to the Old Coke formula under the name Coca-Cola Classic, along with the slogan, "You can't beat the real thing." In the early nineties, they changed their slogan to "Always Coca-Cola." They said that they had to let people know that it would always be Coca-Cola. There was a resurgence of interest in the product.

You should strive to be better. However, you should be yourself in the process. You can change your hair color, or it may fall out, your weight can fluctuate, your income can change, you may drive a different car, live in a different neighborhood, find a better job, become more than what you have been, but stay true to who you are. That is ultimately where true success lies.

Accepting the Challenges

"The true measure of a man is not how he behaves in comfort and convenience, but rather controversy and challenge."
-Martin Luther King Jr.

While you are getting better and moving toward the fulfillment of your purpose, there will always be challenges. However, if you are to win at anything, those challenges must be accepted. You cannot shy away from the challenges in your life. You must learn to accept and defeat those challenges.

Michael Jordan and his team, before winning their sixth NBA championship, were up three games to two on the Utah Jazz. They had to play the remaining two games on the road at the hostile Utah Jazz arena against fellow Hall of Famers Karl Malone and John Stockton. During a press conference, Jordan was asked about going back to Utah to try to win the championship. He looked at the reporter and said, "I accept the challenge." During the final few seconds of the game, he stole the ball from Karl Malone, dribbled down the court, waved everyone away, put a move on his defender, hit the game winning shot, and ultimately won his final championship.

Tiger Woods, in the 2001 Players Championship, which went to a tiebreak with a lesser-known opponent, was asked about the pressure and the hype surrounding the event and how it might affect his game. Tiger said, "I accept the challenge." He went out and won the championship.

Space Shuttle Discovery launched its historic return to flight mission, two-and-a-half years after the tragic space shuttle Columbia accident. The flight was a monumental success. Pilot Jim Kelly was asked his reasons for performing this mission. He said, "I enjoy the challenge."

Walter Payton, the great Chicago Bears running back, used to say that he would rather dish out punishment than take it. So many times defenders would come to tackle him only to find that he was lowering his shoulder and helmet into their chests first. He was not very big, and by all accounts he was not very fast, but he enjoyed the challenge.

Chappie James, who became the first black to attain the rank of four-star full general and commander of the North American Air Defense Command (NORAD), said that his mother always told him that if a fight was inevitable then he should be the one to start it.

You see, sometimes we sit around and allow things to happen to us instead of taking on the events and challenges in our lives. Challenges must be accepted and met head-on if you expect to defeat them.

The Hawk and the Swan

The tortoise walks up to the swan and asks, "Why are you crying?" The tortoise says, "Oh I see why you are crying, it's the hawk isn't it? He has picked out your eye." The swan says, "But

Mr. Tortoise that's not why I'm crying. I am crying because I let him... because I let him."

How many of us allow others to make us feel bad? How many people allow their bosses or friends to make them feel inferior? You should not hang around people who make you feel bad, and tell you that you are ugly, fat, or stupid. Do not give people the power to control how you feel, act, and behave. We sometimes behave as if we need a puppeteer. If you need someone to pull your strings, there is no shortage of people who will line up for the job. You should never believe that you are second rate even if you are a bit behind. Do not be afraid to challenge a situation even though it may seem impossible.

The Underdog

There are times when all appears lost or you are way behind, but that does not mean that you will not win. You do not have to be the favorite. In fact, all of us like stories of the underdog. We all like stories of people who rose from the bottom to the top. We do not want to hear about the person who was on top their whole life. We want to hear about the underdog, like Jennifer Hudson. We fell in love with her because she lost American Idol, but came back and gave an Academy-Award-winning performance among an all-star cast in the movie Dream Girls. The same people who did not vote for her on American Idol instantly started to love her. It is because we all can relate to her story. We fall in love with people who have qualities we can see in ourselves. We all have lost and are looking for that big break.

We should always look for the pot of gold at the end of the rainbow. We must always believe that we are a diamond in the rough. We will always be intrigued by the story of Cinderella, whose stepmother and step-sisters treat her unfavorably for years, but is later chosen as princess. We like the story of the race between the tortoise and the hare because the tortoise wins, regardless of his unfavorable odds. We all have read about the frog that was kissed and became a prince. The person who wins the lottery is always the subject of conversation around the water cooler. We are intrigued by how much the person won, but more intrigued by what they were doing before they won. We like to hear stories about the truck driver, struggling single mother of five, coal miner, or factory worker who comes up with a great idea or invention that becomes a success.

We like these rags-to-riches stories because they are about regular people with whom we can relate. They seem to give us hope. Which story is more intriguing—Bill Gates making another ten million dollars because Microsoft's stock soared yesterday—or a struggling waitress who finally gets her long awaited recording contract. The struggling waitress would win every time.

We all have some Cinderella, some tortoise, some frog, or a bit of Jennifer Hudson in us. We all have been down and out. We all have been in the back. Now it is time for us to win. You must understand that you do not have to just dream. Your dreams can come true. Your wishes can become reality.

People will only scoff at you when you keep thinking that you can make your dreams come true. Only when you are trying to do more with your life will people scorn you. As soon as you discuss your business plan with people who are losers and broke-and-choke thinkers, they will shoot your idea down before they ever hear your message. Their idea for something better is for you to go away and not embarrass yourself and others with your wacky ideas. If at least one person does not think that your dream is too lofty, then you are not dreaming big enough. What if at the age of five, LeBron James told someone that he would score 5,000 points quicker than anyone else would in the history of the NBA? People would have told him he was nuts. Some people said, even when he was taken as the first pick in the NBA draft, that he could never live up to the billing. So much for naysayers.

What if Kelly Clarkson, the first American Idol winner, would have announced to the world a year before she appeared on the show that she would have a #1 hit song? They would have said, "But you do not even have a record deal yet, you have never performed in front of a large crowd, you do not have a band, or any backup singers." People would have explained to her all the reasons why she would fail.

People usually tell you that you are nuts because they only see you through their eyes. They want you to hang around and be like them because they have no ambition. The people who do not feel good about themselves are great at one thing and that is throwing pity parties. And guess what? You are always invited and they want you to Bring Your Own Bad Stories (B.Y.O.B.S.), so everyone can sit around and get drunk off them. There will be plenty of other invited guests, such as Mr. Past, Ms. Fear, Mr. Negative Outlook, and Ms. Failure. They all will be there plus many more. You need to tell them that you are busy and cannot make it; you need to tell them that you definitely do not have any bad stories to bring, nor do you want to hear theirs.

Cycle of Poverty

People that have a negative outlook on life are usually caught up in a vicious cycle. It often runs deep into their family history. The cycle is difficult to break. If you are in this cycle, your fight will be twice as hard. You will have to fight not only for you, but also for those in your family and people in your inner circle. You will be, more often than not, the only person in your circle with vision. Do not look for everyone to share your vision because poverty is built deep into a person's psyche. They will ridicule you, and some will even laugh at you, but you must understand that they have an impoverished mentality. So do not get upset with family members and friends who may not ever share your vision. You must love them and move on. Listening to the foul thinking of family members will cause you to give up and fail quicker than any obstacle that you will ever face because these are people you care about and who hold opinions that you value. You must remember that they do not know what you know, feel what you feel, or see what you see. Thus, keep moving ahead in the face of shame and ridicule. Know who you are before they start to shoot at you. After success comes, they will all line up and say they always knew that you would succeed.

Chapter 7: The Six Golden Nuggets of Success

*"The successful person has the habit
of doing the things failures don't
like to do. They don't like doing
them either necessarily, but their
disliking is subordinated to the
strength of their purpose."*

- M. Gray

Nugget#1

Do not wait until you are perfect.

"Don't wait. The time will never be just right."

-Napoleon Hill

Legendary football coach Bobby Bowden of Florida State University used to speak to us all the time about being role models and giving back to the community. His messages were simple. He believed that all of his players should give back in any way we could; whether coaching, mentoring, or speaking. He believed that it was our duty. His motto was that we should not wait until we were perfect. He would say, "If you wait until you are perfect then you'll never do anything."

You do not have to wait until all the stars are lined up before you do something. I have always felt like I had to wait until all my ducks were in a row before I got started. Sometimes if we actually do something, we surprise others and ourselves in the process. How many times have we seen famous athletes, actors, or entertainers say never in their wildest dreams did they think that they would be so successful?

Just do it. Get it done. Start the project, and the rest will work itself out. Many people will never start anything because they fear disaster or failure. Do not worry about what others think of you. You must remember that you do not have to be anything for anyone for any reason.

Nugget #2

You control your own destiny.

"Sow a thought, and you reap an act; sow an act, and you reap a habit; sow a habit, and you reap a character; sow a character, and you reap a destiny."

-Charles Reade

Some things are meant to be, but I believe that based on what you believe and what you are willing to do, you control your own destiny. I will prove it. When you finish reading this sentence, put the book down and clap your hands three times. Did you do it? Were you successful? Whether you performed the exercise or not, you controlled the act of clapping your hands. You made a decision either to follow the directions or not. It was totally up to you. It is still totally up to you. Okay, so you are one of the people that did not do the exercise? I will give you another chance. Put the book down and clap your hands three times. You see, just like the simple act of clapping your hands, you are in control of your life as well.

This is the same as acting on your goals and dreams. You control whether you will or you will not. It is not up to anyone else. It is up to you. You decide what you will become. Your past, your family's history, and where you are from do not matter at this point. Once you walk into the understanding that it is up to you, then you will understand that there is something you can do to make your life what you want it to be.

I get so sick of people talking about what happened in their past. Everyone has a sob story about their past - either about relationships, misfortunes, or origins. No one cares about you or where you are from. No one cares if you are young or old, or if you came from the ghetto or Hollywood Hills. When you present yourself or your business, you will have to show that you and your services are an asset. It does not matter if you have an MBA from Harvard or street cred from L.A. The question will be, can you get the job done? Do you have the knowledge that people are looking for? Do you have the skills that will help advance people's objectives? You must stop focusing on those things that you cannot control and start focusing on those things that you can. Reinhold Niebuhr said it like this, "God grant me the serenity to accept the things that I cannot change, courage to change the things that I can, and the wisdom to know the difference."

Nugget #3

Infinite Momentum.

"Success comes from taking the initiative and following up... persisting... eloquently expressing the depth of your love. What simple action could you take today to produce a new momentum toward success in your life?"

-Tony Robbins

You must understand that momentum is important in every aspect of your life. It is vital to your success. Momentum is the point where the ball gets rolling and you cannot stop it even if you tried. It is also referred to as "critical mass," which is the point when a nuclear reactor can sustain its reaction without additional fuel. When your business reaches critical mass, you had better watch out because it will grow without you being there. To reach this point you have to go crazy: calling prospects, meeting people, showing and talking about your product and service. You have to stay up late at night and rise early the next morning. You have to have unbelievable belief in what you are doing. Only when you do this will you reach some momentum in your business.

Once this momentum comes, you will not be able to stop the prospects from coming to you or stop people from wanting to be a part of what you are doing. People will stand in line just to counsel with you. You had better make certain that you have enough gigabytes of transfer for your website, because even your counter will not be able to keep up with the hits. You had better make sure your publisher and printing company can fill all of the orders for your book because it is about to fly off the shelves. Your speaking engagements will shoot through the roof. Requests will come in by the hundreds. Your schedule will be so full that you may even have to turn down an appearance on Oprah. Okay, maybe not!

Nugget #4

Freedom is not free.

"A champion is someone who gets up when he can't."
-Jack Dempsey

Freedom is not free. If you want to be free, you will have to do something to gain that freedom. America is a place of tremendous opportunity, but it is not free and it never will be. I thank God for troops that continue to fight for our country and the people in it. We all should be truly grateful for what they do because they allow us the opportunity to live extraordinary lives, but it is not free. Many of the soldiers have been permanently injured both mentally and physically. Some have even paid the ultimate sacrifice fighting for the freedoms that we enjoy. After watching a CSPAN special on the Walter Reed Army Medical Center and seeing what injured soldiers go through after returning home from war, I became even more thankful for the freedoms that we enjoy and more grateful for what our soldiers do. There can never be enough done to show them that we appreciate their services. The special presentation reemphasized the fact that we should never take our freedoms for granted. There are those who always have to make sacrifices so that others can live and enjoy the freedoms that we share.

I am careful not to compare our life's aspirations to the real battlefield that soldiers fight on, but you will not enjoy freedom in your life without some personal sacrifices. If you think that you will be able to come up with an idea, quit your job, walk in a bank and secure a business loan, and waltz into a flourishing business, you are in for a rude awakening. If you think that you won't have to kick in some doors to be noticed, then you had better talk to some successful people. If you think that people will help you because you look pitiful, then your lips will always hang to the ground. There will be a price to pay for an extraordinary life. There will always be a story to tell. Freedom will never be free.

Which one of the following speeches sounds more like a championship speech?

Championship Speech #1

I wrote the acceptance speech for our team at the beginning of the season because all year long we were the favorites. Everyone predicted that we would win the championship. We just cruised through the season without any problems. No one ever doubted us. We were the favorites from start to finish. We have had nothing but positive reinforcement from day one. Our competitors did not compete against us very hard because they knew they had no chance of winning. We did not put in any extra time practicing, or studying our mistakes, or the strategies of our opponents. It was not difficult at all and this championship came very easily. I do not think that any of us, including the coaches, ever lost any sleep. In fact, this was not even a dream of ours, but it happened anyway.

Championship Speech #2

People doubted us all year. We had to overcome injuries, ailments, bumps, and bruises. We had some tough decisions to make, but we made them. We had to believe in ourselves when no one else did. We had a good team, but the difficult part was putting everything together. Everyone had to be on the same page. We endured hard-fought competition from our competitors. They were on our heels the whole way, but we just kept fighting and pushing. On many days, my teammates and I wanted to quit, but we decided to stick it out. We are all exhausted beyond belief, but all the hard work and dedication has finally paid off.

Of course, Speech #2 sounds like every acceptance speech ever uttered; so why would your story be any different? Why do people, when they find out how much work is required, baulk at the idea of moving on?

People are going to laugh at you and doubt you. There will be mountains and hills to climb. The critics will be out on every corner. Country music star Toby Keith said, "You should never listen to critics because you're never that good and you're never that bad." Trust me, if your acceptance speech is like Speech #1, I guarantee that you have not accomplished much.

Nugget #5

Do not compare.

*"I am more and more convinced that our happiness or unhappiness
depends more on the way we meet the events of life than on the
nature of those events themselves."*

-Alexander Humboldt

People will always remind you of your family tree, especially
if those found within its branches are infamous or have notorious
reputations. You will hear such statements as: the apple does not
fall far from the tree; you will be just like your worthless father;
your mother was a crack addict so you will be one also. These
utterances could not be further from the truth. There are plenty
of stories of how people pulled themselves out of the slums and
poor houses only to find themselves in downtown penthouses
and mansions.

Yes, it is true that the apple does not fall far from the tree, but
it does fall off, perhaps, after realizing that it no longer belonged
on the tree. Some apples fall, others are picked, and the rest are
knocked out of the tree, but for whatever reason, they are no
longer attached to the tree. When someone says that you will
be like someone else in your lineage, tell him or her that you are
proud to be from that tree, but you are not attached to it any
longer.

Nugget #6

Betrayal.

"A man who doesn't trust himself can never really trust anyone else."
-Cardinal De Retz

Who has betrayed you more than anyone else? Who has made and broken promises to you more than anyone else? Who is it that you cannot and do not trust? What would you like to do to this person? What would you say to them if you could speak your mind without any consequences? You must take all those negative emotions and feelings, bottle them up, and then let them go. Why? Because the one person who has betrayed you the most, lied to you, and said discouraging things to you more than anyone else is YOU!

How many times have you betrayed yourself? How many times have you lied to yourself? How many times have you told yourself that you were going to go on a diet and it did not happen? You have told yourself repeatedly that you were going to quit your bad habits and you have not. In addition, you wonder why doubts set in when you are about to undertake a challenge. You wonder why you do not believe in yourself. You even hate yourself for this betrayal, distrust, and disloyalty. You are the one who goes around wishing that you were someone else, hating to look in the mirror, shying away from making any more promises, New Year's resolutions, or setting any goals.

You must step over yourself if you want to ever get on in life. You must forgive yourself if you ever want to get out of the trap of insecurity and doubt. So stop betraying yourself if you want to step in the fulfillment that you know is yours. James Whitaker, the first American to reach the summit of Mt. Everest, after enduring dehydration, hypothermia, avalanches, and much fatigue, said, "You don't conquer the mountain, you conquer yourself."

It is not the issues or people in your life that are holding you back. It is you! The mountain is not as big as it looks when you conquer you first.

To help conquer yourself and subsequently those huge mountains in your life, you need to start by conquering molehills. Coach Prig used to say that it is the little things in life that count the most. You need to start making some small commitments first and then progress. Try going to the gym three times this week for one hour. Get up early enough to spend some time in thought for a change. Make a promise that you are going to eat healthy, even if it kills you, one day this week. (It may defeat the purpose if it kills you!) You need to make at least one call that you have been procrastinating about within the next two weeks. As you start to keep your commitments, your attitude and confidence in yourself will start to rise. This will ultimately help you start believing in yourself more, thus giving you what you need to attempt the bigger goals and dreams that you have.

Chapter 8: Focus

"You can't do anything about the length of your life, but you can do something about its width and depth."

- Shira Tehrani

A little black boy goes to a carnival. He sees a clown blowing up balloons and releasing them. He sees a white one, a blue one, a green one, and finally a yellow balloon being released. They all soar high into the sky. He then asks the clown if a black balloon would go as high. The clown, seeing the sense of bewilderment on his face, takes a black balloon out of his bag, fills it with helium, and releases it into the air. To the little boy's amazement, it soars higher than all the other balloons. The clown turns to the boy and says, "It's not what's on the outside, but what's on the inside that counts."

Gatorade has a slogan that says, "Is it in you?" What is inside you will determine what you will become. It is the positive influences, affirmations, and messages to which you listen. It is the fears that you conquer and bad thoughts of which you rid yourself. It is the courage that you muster and the hope onto which you hold.

You must develop the belief that everything you need is inside you. Tony Robbins said, "Your beliefs determine what you are willing to try or not try, what you are willing to do or not do…they could either be the keys to your freedom or they could be the giant locks to the prisons that keep you from getting what you want." Walt Disney said, "Somehow I can't believe that there are any heights that can't be scaled by a man who knows the secret of making dreams come true. This special secret, it seems to me, can be summarized in four C's. They are curiosity, confidence, courage, and constancy, and the greatest of these, confidence. When you believe in something, believe in it all the way - implicitly and unquestionably."

You must be convicted in your beliefs to achieve optimum results. Can you see a correlation between your beliefs and what you have attempted in the past? If you could, wouldn't you go back and change the beliefs you had? If you changed those beliefs then invariably your actions would've changed, conceivably changing the desired results.

The only belief that some people have is in their own self-doubt. They only believe that things do not. They only believe in the possibility of failures. They only believe in the reasons why most people must be broke for others to be rich. They only believe in the "cannots," and doubt the "cans."

Be careful because doubt is very persuasive. Doubt can lead you to the best answers. When you sit with doubt and listen to all of its reasons why you cannot perform a task, you will start to believe what doubt has to say.

I was listening to my mother speak to a group of people when she quoted a scripture from the Bible which read, "All things are possible to him that believe." (Mark 9:23) I read the scripture and it jumped out at me. It says nothing about your background, educational level, race, size, or any other issues that we get hung up on. It has only to do with your level of belief. Most of us have the talent. In fact, we have more talent than we need. We just need help with our belief. There are people who are less talented in your field, but have more belief in themselves and subsequently have had more success to this point. There are actors and actresses who believe in their abilities enough that they audition for every part they can. There are singers who will stop at nothing to get the label's decision makers to listen to their music in hopes of getting a record deal.

Robert F. Kennedy said, "Few will have the greatness to bend history itself, but each of us can work to change a small portion of events… It is from numberless acts of courage and belief that human history is shaped."

You must live your life as though everything is possible, if only you believe. You must walk into the understanding and believe that it truly is all inside. We all could use a boost in the belief department.

Commitment

Solid beliefs will birth solid commitments based on those beliefs. You cannot be driven in anything unless you are committed. Some people cannot commit to anything. There are people who cannot commit to a lane to drive in while in traffic without questioning their decision. People do not commit because they do not want to be considered a failure if they are wrong. As I have stated, you have to be willing to live with the decisions that you make.

On sports talk shows, very often the analysts have to choose the team that they feel will win. Retired football player turned commentator, Michael Irvin, said that that is what they are paid to do, give an opinion and pick a winner. How frustrating it would be if every sportscaster during each broadcast said, "I do not know what will happen or who will win the game; it could go either way. I think I'll just wait until the game is over to pick a winner." What if you went to your stockbroker and asked his opinion about which stocks to invest and he said to you, "I do not know. What do you think? Your guess is just as good as mine." If this is the only answer that he can muster, then he is not going to be in business very long. We gravitate to people who have an opinion and a position. People will not follow you if you are not committed.

Donald Trump's show, The Apprentice, would not be as popular if he was indecisive about whom to hire or fire. He has to make up his mind after each boardroom visit and say to someone, "You're fired!" I have often heard him say, "She was great, but I can live with my decision." When you make a commitment, you are making a decision to do or not do. Once you have made the decision, you must be willing to reap the benefits and/or suffer the consequences.

In basketball you often see players, after missing a few shots, become hesitant to shoot. They almost never hit the shot when they hesitate. In auto-racing, drivers and teams have to make several decisions and commitments to the strategies they will use. Once a driver makes a commitment to pass, he has to step on the gas and go for it. A fraction of a second could be the difference between an accident and a victory lap. Once they commit to not taking a pit stop, then it is off to the finish line. Often times you hear that a driver has won the race on fumes.

Once you commit to it, then you must stay motivated through it. You must be motivated through your commitments. Once you get a plan of action and a goal in mind, you must commit yourself to it. You must be motivated through everything that happens from that point forward. You must understand that there will be tough times, difficult situations, and unfortunate events. Vincent Lombardi said, "The quality of a person's life is in direct proportion to their commitment to excellence, regardless of their chosen field of endeavor."

Be committed to it and motivated through it, while at the same time remaining attentive. There will be times when you will have to alter your course midstream. In football, when one team has the ball and it changes possession, either by interception, fumble, blocked kick, or some other action, it is referred to as sudden change. During sudden change, defensive players are now trying to score and offensive players are trying to defend against the score. There is no time to bring tackling specialists on the field for one team or blocking and running specialists on the field for the other. Each player has to adapt to his environment and perform tasks that he is not used to performing.

In driving school, you are taught to be a defensive driver. If someone runs a red light and comes in your direction, you have to be able to react quickly and change course to prevent an accident. The same rings true in life. Often times you will not be able to follow the given path in a robotic manner.

I believe that most people are not slobs. I believe that most people are not lazy jerks, but rather things happen to them that are beyond their control. There is sudden change.

One incident can change your life. It could be your accountant telling you that your company has serious tax issues and the IRS is knocking at your company's door. The police may have come to you with news of a loved one who has passed. It could be a loss of employment due to a lay-off. Maybe you have waited your whole life to have kids only to be told by your doctor that you have had a miscarriage and having kids is no longer possible. You get news of an incurable illness. Your husband dies and you are left with all the expenses. Your boss cuts your hours and your check is not as much as it should have been. Thus, you cannot cover your expenses. Your wife leaves you in the middle of the night with the kids. Your favorite coach quits mid-season. Your top mechanic takes ill. The starting quarterback gets hurt. Your partner takes the money out of the business account and leaves you with no cash and all the creditors knocking at your door.

Any of these events could devastate your life and take you over the edge or off the deep end. You must already have a positive perspective about your life. You must do everything possible to take advantage of the life that you are now living. You could be a perfectly sane person today and tomorrow one event or bad circumstance could have you staring out the window of a mental hospital, taking more drugs in one week than you have taken in a lifetime. Do not worry, but understand that life is short. Taking advantage of the life you have now is one of the most important things you can do. James Allen said, "Circumstances don't make a man, they reveal him." Each event in your life will bring out who you really are inside. It will reveal if you are strong and committed or if you just have an inflated ego.

I used to say to myself when I was training heavily that hard work was my best friend, but consistency was my worst enemy. In your pursuit, you will have to be persistently consistent. Your persistence will drive you past the difficult times in your life.

Calvin Coolidge said, "Nothing will take the place of persistence. Talent will not; nothing is more common than unsuccessful people with talent. Genius will not; unrewarded genius is almost a proverb. Education will not; the world is full of educated derelicts. Persistence and determination alone are omnipotent."

If a person works hard at sales and never gets a sale and quits within a week, he cannot be considered persistent and consistent. Many people persist for far too short a time. You must make your efforts consistently persistent. You must continue to look for investors for your company or prospects for your network marketing business. This process may take more time and effort than you had previously imagined. Everyone has to pay a price to be successful. Do not compare yourself to others. Your price will always be different from someone else's. You should do whatever you have to do to get the results you are looking for.

George Bernard Shaw said, "People are always blaming their circumstances, the people who get on in this world are the people who look for the circumstances that they want and if they can't find them they make them."

Have you made any circumstances that you want today? Have you made any opportunities that you want? What are some of the circumstances and opportunities you need to live a better life? You need to start looking for those circumstances and opportunities, and if you can't find them, make them.

Henry Ford is a great example of someone who created circumstances. At the time, he figured out the most efficient way to mass produce the automobile, by way of the assembly line, however, there was not a huge demand for cars. Some people believed that cars were useless because everyone worked, went to school, visited, and shopped close to where they lived. People rarely traveled to other destinations. Today, in many places people are considered close if they can get to work within an hour's time. We also use our cars for vacations, nights out, cruising, and just showing off. Like Mr. Ford, you may have to create the product or service, and the need for it too.

Switching Gears

While you are being persistently consistent, creating a need for your product or service and looking for circumstances that will take you to the next level, you have to keep it all in perspective. While you may be riddled with the prospect of your career and future endeavors, you need to understand that balance in your life is just as important. If your life is not balanced, then your life will ultimately sink because your boat is too heavy on one side. To be balanced, you have to have the ability to switch gears.

Some people work all day and bring their jobs home with them - whether it is talking about what happened at work or being in a bad mood because something during the day did not go as planned. There is nothing wrong with having a conversation about your career. If you are committed to what you are doing, there will always be some discussion, but switching gears means that you have to be able to switch from negotiating a multi-national multi-million dollar deal with top executives all over the world, to having a conference with your daughter's third grade teacher. You have to go from managing a huge construction project and supervising hundreds of employees, to coming home and taking out the garbage. You have to go from running all day, reading scripts, being in and out of cabs, and speaking with major network executives, to reading to your child. You have to be able to complete an architectural drawing by the deadline for your company's most important client, to waking up and following your pre-planned schedule of going to the gym. People who can switch gears will have balance and stability in their lives.

Back to the Mountain Top

If your life has become out of balance, all is not lost. You can get back to the times when you had balance and you were blazing the trails of success. You can win again. If it has been done once, it can be done again.

One thing that Muhammad Ali said when he started training again in an effort to win his third heavyweight title, was that he had to go back to the mountaintop and shock the world again. He said, "To win, all I have to do is suffer." You must do the same. You must stay in attack mode. You must conquer the demons that exist inside you before you regain the balance necessary for success to come. You must get back to the mountain top.

I have had a myriad of speaking experiences to countless groups of diverse people, in places you would not imagine. During one memorable occasion, I was invited to speak at a halfway house to about twelve men who were all recovering crack addicts. I was uneasy about this engagement because I did not think that I had the ability to relate to them. However, with my take-on-the-challenge attitude, I decided that it would be a good experience for me, and maybe I could share something that could help them.

When I arrived, the first thing that I noticed was that none of the men had any expression on their faces. They all had blank stares. They had arranged the chairs in a circle as though that is how they thought that I should present. They were all ten to fifteen years older than I. They were intelligent, articulate, and had experienced just about everything that life has to offer. They were in a court ordered facility. Most of them did not have family or friends outside of the people in the house. They had allowed their habit to take control of their lives and no one trusted them any longer; furthermore, their friends and families rejected their very existence. They had hit rock bottom and I knew that I was going to have to come up with something better than a "rah, rah" you-can-do-it speech to touch them.

I began to share with them and allowed them to share with me. My goal was to have them view their lives as though they were watching it on a big screen in a movie theater. I wanted them to understand that there would be more pain associated with relapsing than there would be pleasure. To do this, I began to ask questions. I asked them to tell me about a time in their lives when they felt their best, were on top of the world, and led productive lives. They agreed and began to share and open up.

As the session was about to come to a close, the second to last man began to speak. He spoke about his family, specifically his daughter. He talked about how even though they did not have much as a family, his daughter, who was about eleven years old at the time, had walked up to him one day, put her arms around him and told him how much she appreciated what he had done for her. She explained that what they did not have did not matter, but what did matter was the fact that she had a loving father. He explained that she went on to state how lucky she was to have a father like him.

Knowing that a daughter can get to a man's heart more than anything, his, and the rest of the men's in the room, eyes filled with tears. There was not a dry eye in the room. After thinking about his past life and realizing what he had seemingly thrown away, he could only shake his head in discontent. He immediately began saying that he was never returning to his former drug induced lifestyle. Although he had not seen his daughter in years, she was the only thing that he believed kept him going.

Other men started to relate to him by recalling situations in their own lives. They began to echo what he related by saying that addiction was not worth losing everything. I thought to myself, easy enough, this is great, I really got through to them. I wanted to end the meeting at that point, but I could not. There was one man who had not told his story. Although there was barely any light in the room, this man wore a pair of sunglasses. He also wore long denim pants, a black t-shirt with a pocket, black dress shoes, white socks, and a baseball cap. Before I could say anything he said, "I believe it is my turn now."

He began to speak in a heavy, booming, and intimidating voice. He said, "You want to know when I felt my best?" I said, "Go ahead, why don't you tell us." He said, "It was when I had money in my pocket, my bills were paid, my crib was laid, I had a sweet ride, women on my arm, a pocket full of money, and I could get all my friends together, throw a party, pay for everything, and we could all get BLITZED! We would just smoke as much crack as we could stand. I would wake up not remembering anything from the night before. I had just had the time of my life again. Now that was when I felt my best."

There came a hush over the room. No one said anything. I was stunned. I couldn't believe it. Everyone there, it appeared, seemed to be in agreement with him, that it sounded like a great night. However, no one said anything. I felt eyes peering at me, saying, now Mr. Speaker Guy, what are you going to say to that? I had several thoughts go through my head. What could I say to this? Was he joking? He is probably telling the truth, I thought. I had to come up with something.

So I defused the situation and agreed with him by telling him that indeed it sounded like a great night. I tried to make a joke by saying I wish I had been there, but it didn't go over very well. So I paused for a moment, then I asked him what he thought were his worst times. He explained that being locked up, sleeping on the streets without food to eat, not seeing his children, and rummaging through garbage cans with the homeless people were some of his lowest moments. As the session proceeded, I tried to show him that those great times ultimately caused his worst times. He gave a slight nod, seemingly cooperating, but not agreeing. I wrapped up my talk. However, when I finished, no one said a word.

As I was leaving, saying my goodbyes, the director said, "Man, they loved you. We've got to have you back." I said, "But they didn't say anything. I figured they hated me." He said, "That's how they respond when they like you. If they didn't think you were good, they would have told you to leave before you were finished. You are one of the best speakers we've ever had."

I learned a very important lesson that day: never ask a question unless you are fully prepared to hear the truth.

If your mountaintop puts you in compromising situations, such as performing unproductive, illegal, and irresponsible acts, then I don't want you to get back to those times. Please leave them where they are. I don't want you to feel that good!

You always see young stars with a world of potential and then they seem to fall off the map. You have probably had potential to do great things at one point your life. Then something happened. Either you experienced a tragedy or you fell upon hard times. There was sudden change. Now it is time for you to get back to the training that will take you from where you are to where you want to be.

For some, it is going back to school to finish that degree. For others, it is rebuilding a failed business and making it successful again. For many, it is rekindling a fire in your relationship that had you and your family on an unstoppable journey. Others have to get back in the studio and record again. It could be beginning to write once more. Maybe you need to rededicate yourself to God. Whatever it is, you have to work to get back to that point. It is going to be difficult. It is going to be hard. It is twice as hard to get back once you have lost the momentum, but do not get discouraged - you can do it. You can make it happen. You should pursue your rekindled goal with all of your might. It does not matter how dim the course looks ahead; turn on your headlights, even your fog lights, and keep moving. It does not matter how you feel, you must be willing to suffer a little. You must get back to your mountaintop and shock the world again.

The Gas Station Education

Some of the most important advice I have ever received, which has helped me balance my life, was given in some of the strangest places. These places include the barbershop, in line at the grocery store, in a restroom, and on an elevator. However, I never expected to receive some of this valuable information at a gas station.

One night during my college days, I was headed home when I decided to pull over for gas. While pumping gas, a man at a pump across from me struck up a conversation. We started to talk about several things, but mostly he talked and I listened. He said, "Young man, I feel I need to give you a bit of advice." I felt compelled to listen even though I had not asked him for any. He said, "Young man when it's late at night, or early in the morning and you have awoken, you should write. You have to write when everyone is asleep. You have to write, write, and write some more. When you wake up, don't turn on the television or go to the refrigerator, but write." We finished pumping our gas and he looked at me and said, "Don't forget to write." He then got in his car and left. I have never seen him again.

I have often reflected on what he said. When I awake, I always try to write. When I do, my day goes smoother and I feel like I am in harmony with the universe. When I do not write during some part of the day, I find myself feeling totally out of balance. Everyone should write at some point during the day. You may be writing a song, memoir, diary entry, or book, or simply updating your goals, but writing will help you release what you have inside. It is therapy for the soul.

Some ten years or so later, I was at a different gas station when I met a gentleman from South Florida. We had a decent conversation about life. He gave me his name and contact information. Sometime later, I called to check in on how he was doing. As the conversation progressed, he started to give me advice. A couple of things he told me really stood out. He said, "To make it to the shore, you've got to row that boat as hard as you can. You may get tired, but you must continue to row. Sometimes you have to change your seating position, but you must continue to row." As I was about to hang up he said, "Hold on young man. The other thing that you must do is read. You must read, read, and read some more. The radio is good and the TV is okay, but reading is most important."

I thought to myself, why is this old man giving me such cliché advice? I can already read, why is he telling me this? Does he not know that I have an education? This advice is surely not for me. As I thought about what he said, I later remembered what the other gentleman had said some ten years earlier. I heeded his advice.

Bill Gates said, "I really had a lot of dreams. I think a great deal of that grew out of the fact that I had a chance to read a lot." General Colin Powell, who was the sixty-fifth Secretary of State of the United States and once the highest ranking African American government official in the history of the United States, said that when he looks back on his life, there was one important thing that he learned at an early age and that was that reading could take him anywhere in the world that he wanted to go. He said that he indulged himself in reading everything that he could get his hands on.

The message is the same; reading is fundamental and writing is therapy for the soul. You should do both on a regular basis to help you balance your life.

Focus

You will not achieve balance in life, nor can you expect to maximize your potential in life, without having extreme focus.

In the movie Ghost, Carl Bruner (Tony Goldwyn) has his friend Sam (Patrick Swayze) killed in an attempt to gain access to fraudulent accounts through which Carl has laundered money. Sam becomes a ghost, but his girlfriend Molly Jensen (Demi Moore) cannot hear, feel, or see him. The only person that knows he exists is a medium, Oda Mae Brown (Whoopi Goldberg). Sam gets Ms. Brown to help him end Carl's plan to gain control over the assets. As the plot thickens, Sam discovers that his friend Carl has figured out where the money has gone and now Sam has to protect Molly. However, he cannot figure out how to help her because everyone except for Ms. Brown cannot feel, hear, or see him.

One day, he is on the subway and a man sees him and begins to yell at him to get off his train. The man is a ghost (Vincent Schiavelli) like Sam. He begins fighting Sam by throwing him against the walls of the train and pounding on him. He even throws things at him. Sam, amazed by what the ghost is able to do, begs the ghost to show him how he performs those feats. He begins to teach Sam how to use his sense of touch by having him kick a can. Sam is unsuccessful at kicking the can for a while. Then the ghost tells him, "You're trying to move it with your finger. You can't push it, you're dead. It's all in your mind, it's all up here! You want to move it with your mind! You've got to focus!" Sam asks him, "How do you focus?" The ghost says, "You take all your energy. You've got to take all your emotions, all your anger, all your love, all your hate, and push it way down into the pit of your stomach, and let it explode like a reactor." Sam, acting on that advice, begins to focus and then succeeds at kicking the can.

Pat Summit, head women's basketball coach at the University of Tennessee and all-time most winning coach in NCAA basketball history, said that the key to her success is her unbelievable focus.

During my final class in graduate school, I had to write one last paper. I was burned out and just ready to get the process over, which resulted in a sub-par paper.

My professor, a 4' 2" older caucasian woman, was not impressed with some of my comments. She looked at me while holding my paper in her hand and shaking it in my face and said, "What is this? This is garbage! This kind of stuff won't make the grade. What are you doing? You have to think! What are you going to do? Your people are worse off today than they were twenty years ago. There are more fatherless black kids than ever. The ghettos and slums are overcrowded. What are you going to do? You have to focus! You have to think! Who's going to do it for you? I hope you're not depending on the government to help you. I hope you are not depending on some social program. That's all a mirage, an illusion, or some fantasy. Those programs are not going to work. I can't help you beyond this point. It's your fight, not mine. It's your problem, not mine. The only advice that I can give you is that you've got to FOCUS!"

When you are trying to succeed, you have to focus. You cannot succeed at anything without unbelievable focus. You have to take all of your emotions, hopes, desires, ambitions, and love, put it in the pit of your stomach, and let it explode like a reactor. You have to believe. You have to want it, feel it, and be it. When this happens, you will be able to kick your can in life.

Lance Armstrong

Lance Armstrong overcame a battle with testicular cancer to win a record-breaking seven consecutive Tour de France Championships. He had a less than fifty-fifty chance to live. Not only did he live, but he will be recorded in history as the best cyclist ever. He said that if it were not for him being diagnosed with cancer, he would not have won the Tour de France. He said, "It taught me to focus. It taught me to fight hard, harder than before. I was a good cyclist already before this, but I was probably on cruise control a little too much. A talented athlete can be on cruise control and still have success, but a talented athlete who attacks every day can be the best."

He had unbelievable focus. He trained to the point where he knew his total body muscle make-up, his maximal oxygen consumption, his heart rate (his heart is thirty percent larger than the average person's), and obviously his weight, sleep patterns, and how his body produces lactic acid. These were just a few of the physical components of his training regimen, not to mention all the other aspects of how and where he trained, and the number of companies who came together to build a perfect bicycle for him.

To me, he embodies everything about motivation, the will to win, never giving up, hope, faith, desire, passion, and commitment. His story is one of a miraculous journey from defeat to victory. Needless to say, he was very focused. How are you doing in the focus department?

Pat Tillman

Pat Tillman secured the last remaining scholarship for Arizona State University in 1994. Years later, he was a seventh round draft pick out of Arizona State University. He ultimately turned down a lucrative NFL contract to enlist in the Army after the 9/11 incident. He had an interview before he left for war and was asked his motivation for enlisting. He said, "My great-grandfather was in Pearl Harbor. A lot of my family have gone and fought in wars and I really haven't done a d*** thing as far as laying myself on the line like that. So I have a great deal of respect for those that have."

Here is a guy that turned down a 3.6 million dollar contract, seemingly at the top of his profession, who felt like there was much more that he needed to do with his life. So he enlisted in the Army to fight for his country. He ultimately gave his life trying to do more with his life than just merely exist. He locked in and focused on what he thought was his ultimate calling.

When you start feeling like you have done a whole lot, I want you to think of Pat Tillman. Look around, and see if there is a greater mission. What is the greater mission for your life? It is ultimately not about how others feel about you, but rather, how you feel about yourself. The Creator has given you certain gifts. People who see you as successful do not share your gifts. They do not know what you know. They do not understand that you have much more to give. When we start listening to others tell us how great we are, we stop growing. When we stop growing, emptiness sets in, and that is when we are headed for the dirt.

You will never be more than what you are by having attitudes like: I got mine, I am better than you are, or I do not need anyone. Almost every day I look at myself and say, I really have not done anything. When I start to think that I have arrived, I will always think of Pat Tillman. In the grand scheme of things, we all have much more to give. We all need to do our part. We all need to give more than what we have been given. We have to say more than what we have been saying. Ultimately, we have got to do more than what we have been doing.

When you start to drift off track, you must remain focused on your ultimate goal. You must keep your focus above everything else.

Chapter 9: People Types

"A man is, but the product of his thoughts what he thinks, he becomes."

- Mahatma Gandhi

I was out of town on a business trip sitting in my hotel room relaxing, when I began to think of all the things I needed to do. A few things came to mind like exercising, reading, and writing. At that point, I remembered that I could not exercise because I had left my running shoes at home. I thought, well maybe I will do some reading. I had some books, but none of them were interesting enough. Finally, I thought I would do some writing, but I could not because I was missing some very important material that I needed, so that was out of the question too.

At that point, my life changed. I started to think about all the things that I had always wanted to do. There were goals that I had set years and years earlier that had never came to fruition. There were problems and situations that I wanted to tackle that I had not because I was sidetracked. I realized that there were millions of people just like me who always wanted to do things like lose weight, start their own businesses, have better relationships, get better jobs, buy homes, have more money in the bank, clean up their credit, and have better health. The dreams that others and I had were only dreams because of the excuses that we had been making.

I was the person who thought that if I was younger, and in college again, I would have learned a new skill or chosen a different major. I heard myself say things like, "when I get more experience I will try to find a better job." I thought to myself, when I feel better, I will start my exercise program. I believed that if I had more money in my savings account, that I would start my own business. I was like everyone else who made these statements of procrastination, fear, and doubt.

As I sat in that dirty, disgusting hotel room, covered with filth, stained linen, and the smell of cigarettes and dried water on the carpet, I became upset at my situation and started to blame everyone else for where I was in my life. As my life flashed before my eyes, I figured that no one was to blame for my situation but me. I was to blame for the amount of money I was making. My weight was the result of my overeating and not exercising. Everything in and out of my life to that point was all because of me.

In an attempt to turn my life around and accomplish some of the goals and dreams that I had set for myself, I came up with categories into which others and I fell. Then I adopted strategies that would help me and others move from these categories to a better life. I refer to these categories as People Types. You may fall into more than one of these categories; most people do. I certainly did. They are:

Causers

The Causers are blamers. They will always find something or someone other than themselves to blame for their current state or circumstances. You will recognize that they may not have the "be" before the "cause." They are good at only one game and that is the blame game. The causers usually blame others or outside forces for the issues that they have. They believe that everything is out of their control. They have an excuse for everything. If they cannot find excuses, they make them up. The causers blame failure on a lack of intelligence, or their height, weight, background, race, environment, or the fact that they do not know the right people, or anything else that they can find.

The ultimate cause for the Causer is God. They say that God did not bless them with the talent, skills, and abilities or that He does not want them to be wealthy or healthy. The Causer will always find a reason for his or her inadequacy. No one can take away the objections from a Causer. He will always find a way to tell you why he cannot. He will never have enough money to do something that improves his life, but will always find a way to buy the 99-inch plasma screen television.

Dr. William Jones, Professor Emeritus at Florida State University, says that therapy is inherent in the diagnosis. Whatever you think the problem is, you will come up with solutions to get rid of that particular problem. If you go to the doctor and he diagnoses your headache as stemming from stress, when in fact you are having an aneurism, he may prescribe an aspirin, when in fact you may need brain surgery.

There is an old story that has been told for quite some time that further illustrates this point. The story is about a man who is outside under a streetlight looking and searching. A friend walks up to him and asks what he is looking for. The searcher explains that he has lost his keys. The friend asks where he last had them.

The searcher tells him that he lost them inside his house. "Why are you outside?" the friend asks. The man says, "Because there is no light in there."

The Causers always look outside themselves in an attempt to locate their problems. They never look at themselves. They take the Myers Briggs personality test and figure they could never amount to much because they were not born a certain type. You can hear the Causer say, "That is just the way I am." They look at the astrological signs that tell them why they do not get along with others and make statements like, "Since I am a Leo, I am not supposed to get along with a Pisces. " Millions of people look at horoscopes, fortune cookies, and the lines in their hands, hoping and wishing that they will tell them something good. Imagine living your whole life based on what is inside a cookie!

The Causer has caused for so long that he cannot get those ideas out of his head. When he starts a new business, such as a clothing line, a network marketing business, or an eBay business, and his wife or best friend reminds him of his past failures, he quits in a hurry. The Causer always believes in the negative. He goes through the vicious cycle of blame. If you ask him the reason he cannot start a business, he will say, "Cause I cannot sell." "Why can't you sell?" "Cause I cannot talk to people." "Why can't you talk to people?" "Cause I am afraid." "Why are you afraid?" "Cause my parents always verbally, and sometimes physically, abused me." "Why did this occur?" "Cause my dad used to drink." "Why did your dad drink?" "Cause he did not have a lot of money." "Why did he not have a lot of money?" "Cause he did not have a good job." The cycle never ends with the Causer. He probably will never do anything, but live from hand to mouth because he will not admit the real reason for his lack of trying. He is afraid, lazy, slothful, and shiftless.

A classic case of "caus'ing" happened during the tragic disaster of Hurricane Katrina. The displaced residents of Louisiana said FEMA did not act quickly enough. FEMA said that they could not deliver the goods because people were shooting at the relief workers. The Governor said it was because the Mayor did not have an evacuation plan. The Mayor said that the Governor and the Federal Government did not give him enough resources. The Government said it was because people did not want to leave the city. Others said it was because the levees were not built or repaired properly. Some felt that God was punishing the city for all of its improprieties. The President said he did not have enough information. Mike Browne, former director of FEMA, quit under fire. Later he testified before the Senate Committee saying that he was just a scapegoat. The headlines the next day read Ex-FEMA Chief Shifts Katrina Blame to DHS (Department of Homeland Security). This was a classic case of caus'ing.

Caus'ing always happens in sports. Causers are the people who bring teams down because they look for improvement everywhere and in everyone else except themselves. The managers, athletic directors, and owners blame the coaches for not motivating the team. The coaches blame management for not giving them adequate time, personnel, or latitude to do their jobs. The offense blames the defense for the other team scoring. The defense blames the offense for turnovers and for leaving them on the field too long. The quarterback blames the offensive line for a lack of protection. The offensive line blames the quarterback for holding on to the ball too long, running into an unprotected area, or calling the wrong play. The receivers blame the quarterback for throwing the ball in double coverage. The quarterback says that the receiver ran the wrong route. The defensive line blames the cornerbacks for allowing the receiver to catch the ball. The cornerbacks say that the defensive line did not put enough pressure on the quarterback and that they cannot cover forever. The safeties blame the linebackers for not helping to cover the receivers. The linebackers blame the safeties for being out of position and not helping to support the run. It never ends.

In businesses, the blaming is not any different. Management blames middle management. Middle management blames the lower level workers who in turn blame all of management.

Caus'ing behaves like an infectious disease and will eat away at the soul of an organization and cause continual failure. Causers should be identified, marked, and sent packing before any team can be successful.

I once was trying to figure out why I had been at the same job for so long. I realized that I had not filled out an application in three years. After I stopped playing the blame game, I filled out an application. Then I started playing the blame game again because I did not get any phone calls. I was amazed as to why I could not get an interview. I started to say things to myself like, "It is because I did not know the right people," and "I was overqualified, or not qualified enough." One day I was reviewing my application and realized that I had not answered the question as to whether I was a U.S. citizen. At the bottom of the application, it read that applications where this question was left blank would be automatically disqualified.

The little oversights in our lives are bigger than we think. Before we start caus'ing, we should look at what we can improve in ourselves. We need to first look at what we can control and then handle those issues. We need to stop looking at the circumstances that are stacked against us. When I fixed my application and resent it, I had three interviews by the end of the following week.

Causers need to look at themselves and see what they can do to make the situation better, instead of blaming others.

Wheners

A Whener sounds like a winner, but they are not. Wheners say things such as, "When I get enough money, I will invest in real estate." They will also espouse fallacies like, "When I lose some weight, I will join the gym, because I am too embarrassed to go to the gym at this point." Wheners are really procrastinators. They will do everything at the last minute. They are huge dreamers who do not have a plan of action. If you are not careful, they will "when" for you and have you waiting on their dreams. When they "when" for others, they say things such as, "When I start my company, I will hire you as the Director of Marketing." This dream never becomes reality. If a Whener does anything significant, they will do more "when'ing" than they ever did before.

Wheners have inflated memories of themselves. They speak of when they were in high school and were the most popular. They tout their past exploits and how they were the greatest at what they did, when they did it. There is usually no evidence of such exploits. Usually the Whener is not even in the team picture, let alone in news clips where he or she averaged twenty-five points per game.

Goners

Goners are going to do everything later. They can be heard saying, "After work, I am going to work in the yard." The difference between Goners and Wheners is that the Goner has a stronger belief in what they are "gon'ing " about. The problem is that they forget to do what they said they would do because they have been saying what they would do for years. Goners have a lot going on in their lives, so much so, that they can hardly remember what is next even though they are surrounded by constant reminders.

Goners are great planners. They buy a Franklin Planner every year. Sometimes they are efficient and only have to buy the inserts. They have calendars on their walls at work and on their refrigerators at home. They have desk calendars and calendars on their phones. They have sticky notes, Post-it notes, and "to do" lists coming out of their ears. However, when it comes to following through with what needs to be done, there is always an excuse.

Goners are master dabblers. They dabble in this and they dabble in that. They never complete anything. They are great at starting and terrible at finishing. They never know what they want at restaurants so they choose the sampler platter. They cannot make sound decisions.

Sooners

Sooners say things such as, "As soon as I do this or that..." They tell their partners, "As soon as I get home, I will help with the kids, we will watch a movie, have dinner, spend some quality time together, and talk about important issues." When the Sooners get home, they eat half of their food, fall back in a lounge chair with remote in hand, and are asleep before they take off their shoes.

Sooners are usually part of management. As a member of management, they make statements like: "As soon as we achieve more of the bottom line, everyone will receive bonuses," or "As soon as we finish this merger, our company will experience exponential growth." Sooners are not forthcoming with their statements. It never fails that something will always come up to keep the Sooner from acting. There will always be some underlying reason that they did not know about before. In reality, the Sooner always creates reasons not to act if there are not any reasons available.

Waiters

The Waiter is not serious about anything. They will ask you to wait until they talk to their partner, brother-in-law, or until they gather more information about your proposition. They make statements such as, "Wait until my ship comes in." Or "Wait until I get my income tax check."

The Waiter always needs one more day. The Waiter feels as though they need to be perfect to start. The truth and fact of the matter is that when they wait on what they have been waiting on, they always wait on something else too.

It is amazing that no matter how many years in a row their team loses, they will always say, "Just wait until next year."

When I was a youngster, my brother and I used to meet our friends at the park to play pick-up basketball. As the park filled with people, the older kids would eventually take our ball and the portion of the court we were playing on and play the full length of the court, leaving us with no place to play. We would often times sit and chat amongst ourselves and say, "Just wait until we are older."

The Waiter will disappear on you. They have good intentions, but we know where the paved road of good intentions leads - to

Hell. They have good hearts and believe that they can get the job done, but doubt always creeps in.

Ifers

Ifers are the people who often feel sorry for themselves. They are great at giving advice, but terrible at taking it. The Ifer's classic statement is, "If I had known then what I know now." The Ifer would have studied harder when they had been in high school or college. They would have married a different person or chosen a different career path. Ifers will not take advantage of an opportunity today just as they did not five, ten, or twenty years ago. Ifers say that they would have loved their loved ones more if they knew that they were not going to be around today, but if you look closely at their lives today, there are people they claim they love, but they never call, e-mail, text, instant message, or write them. An Ifer has a bunch of excuses, but will never admit that that is all they are. Unlike the Wheners, who tell of their past greatness, the Ifers like to tell of their past mistakes. They are willing, at the drop of a hat, to tell their story in hopes that someone will feel sorry for them.

Ifers would have invested in Microsoft years ago. Ifers would have bought the land across the street if they had known then what they know now. Ifers would have taken more chances in life years ago.

Quincy is a small town in Florida about a half an hour from Tallahassee. It was widely believed at one time that there were more millionaires from Coca Cola stock in that city than anywhere else in the world. It has been known for decades as "The Coca Cola town." Early in the century, Mark W. (Mr. Pat) Munroe, President of The Quincy State Bank, thought the Coca Cola Company was well managed and people would always find a nickel for a cold drink, so he began purchasing stock and urged families, friends, and bank patrons to save and invest. By following his advice, many families became financially secure. Some people took advantage of the opportunity and others did not. Unbelievably, there remain people, thirty, forty, and fifty years later who are still saying if they had known then what they know now, they would have invested in the company.

Ifers are great at relationship counseling, but cannot apply the same advice to their own relationships. Either they are never in a relationship or the one that they are in is in disarray.

Steve Martin said, "If you want to know how to be a millionaire, first get yourself a million dollars." How is it that everyone without money knows what to do with it better than those with it? Ifers never think that they have enough money to start a business or create wealth. This is not true. There are several industries where little money is required to get started and a person can amass a fortune.

One such industry is network or multilevel marketing. I am a proponent of this industry because the monetary investment to start is small. Most of the investment will come in the form of time, courage, belief, hope, desire, patience, and commitment. A person can change his destiny just by finding a great company and not quitting. Mark and Rene Yarnell stated in their book, *Your First Year in Network Marketing,* that they have not known anyone who stayed with a solid company for ten or more years who did not become wealthy beyond their wildest expectations. Donald Trump and Robert Kyiosaki have also championed this industry in their book, Why We Want You to Be Rich. In my research I have found that the advantages of being with a great company provides just as many intrinsic rewards as extrinsic rewards. I was not signed on with a company when I started this project, but there is a good chance that I will be signed on with a company by the time it is completed.

Ifers do more wishing than anything. They wish that they were taller so that they could have played in the NBA. They wish that they could sing so that they could have made a record. They say that if they had his talent, or her connections, then they would do this or that. Unless the Ifers stops "if'ing" and acts on the talent and abilities that God has granted them, they will never achieve any goals or dreams in their lives. They will be if'ing until the day they are lowered into the ground.

Thinkers

"The Great Thinker" was a statute sculptured by Auguste Rodin. If you see a picture of this sculptured figure, he just sits there with his fist on his chin, thinking. He probably has some great ideas, but those ideas will never become reality because all he is able to do is think. There are people who are good at going through their hour of power, their daily meditations, and writing down their goals. However, when it is time for action, all they do is think about it. They are great at remembering frivolous information. They become upset with you if you cannot remember or do not know such junk. They have thought of everything that has ever happened, but it is usually after the fact. Then they say, "I told you so." They have predicted everything from Super Bowl winners, World Series winners, to who would be the MVP, but no one remembers it but them. If they are right once, they will remind you forever without ever mentioning the fact that they are one for fifty in their predictions.

When you call them they say, "I was just thinking of calling you."

Thinkers are thinking today and they will be thinking ten years from now. You had better not give the Thinker a business proposal. He will think about it forever. The Thinkers think that they know everything. They lack initiative, drive, ambition, and courage. They have fear of failure, rejection, and what others may think about them, so they mask these fears with thinking things over forever.

If you ask if you can count on them they say, "I think so." When you hear these words, just forget about them. They pray for opportunity but when it comes they say, "Well let me pray about it some more." They use praying to mask the fear of acting.

A man was fishing. His boat developed a hole and began to sink. As he began to sink, he prayed and asked God to rescue him. As he prayed, a boat came by with a possible rescuer and asked if he needed help. The man told the rescuer that he was waiting on God. This sequence of events happened two more times. The man ended up drowning and going to Heaven. He questioned God about what had happened, explaining that he had prayed to him to be rescued. God explained to him that it was him who had sent the rescue boats his way.

You should not rush into decisions and you should think about what you are doing before you do it; but your thinking should be results-oriented and not a mask for procrastination.

Donors

Donors do not know anything. Nothing matters to the Donors. If you ask a Donor what he wants for dinner or what he wants to do later, he will say he does not know and furthermore, he does not care. Many people are very successful in life, but are Donors. If you ask the successful Donor how much he paid in taxes last year, he does not know. If you ask him about his return on investments, he cannot tell you. He does not know how much his agent is making or how the company is doing financially. Be careful because once the Donor becomes important, you will not be able to speak with him directly; you will have to speak to his personal assistant. Donors are headed for trouble. They do not have a clue.

Los Angeles Lakers great, Kareem Abdul Jabbarr, got into financial trouble during the end of his playing career, because he listened to some bad investment advice from someone very close to him. Although he is an intelligent person, he took advice from someone without doing his own research or asking any questions. He lost a ton of money. Willie Nelson fell into the same trap. He got in trouble with the IRS because he listened to the wrong people, or the right people with the wrong advice. Countless other affluent and intelligent people have had this happen to them too.

Donors do not do any research. They place too much trust in the people around them. They turn over decision-making and power of attorney to people they hardly know. They do not know how much is coming in or going out. Donors do not know how much they pay in interest on their credit cards, their home, their cars, or anything of the sort. They are just so excited to get something new that they never read the fine print. They do not know if they have a fixed or a variable rate until they get the notice of foreclosure. Donors do not ever check their credit report until they try to make a purchase and are turned down. They believe that "don'ing" excuses them from blame. It is like the Enron fiasco; the CEO stated that he did not know the company's profits were being overstated, and ended up receiving a huge jail sentence. Donors cannot remember anything of importance. They conveniently forget everything, but what they are supposed to remember.

The Donors do not know how their kids are doing in school. They do not know what goes on in the bedrooms of their kids who live in their home. They do not know the date of their wedding anniversary or their wife's birthday, and they end up sleeping on the front steps for two weeks.

Complainers

Complainers will find anything about which to complain. A man had two sons. One was negative and the other positive. In an attempt to understand each child's attitude, the father decided to perform an experiment. During his experiment, he placed them in separate rooms. He put the positive son in a room full of manure and the negative son in a room full of toys of all kinds. He left them in their respective rooms for an hour. When he came back to see how the kids were doing he found the negative son in the room full of toys complaining. He complained that there were too many toys from which to choose. He complained that some of the toys were too noisy and some were too big. When the father went into the positive son's room, he found him throwing manure all over the walls, jumping in it, playing in it, and having a good time. The parent asked him how he could be having such a good time with all of the manure everywhere. The positive son said, "In a room this size with this much manure there must be a pony around here somewhere." Now that is having a positive attitude!

You should flash this on your computer screen at work, "THERE MUST BE A PONY AROUND HERE SOMEWHERE." Therefore, when you are having a rough day and your place of employment is testing your patience, you can read this message and smile.

Some people will complain about anything and everything. Tori Amos said, "Our generation has an incredible amount of realism, yet at the same time it loves to complain and not really change. Because if it does change, then it won't have anything to complain about."

I went to a friend's house and as I began to enter, I saw a dog lying on the porch moaning and groaning. When my friend came to the door, I greeted him and then asked him why his dog was moaning and groaning. He said, "He's lying on a nail." I said, "Well, why won't he move?" My friend said, "It doesn't hurt him bad enough to move, just bad enough to complain about it."

Some people are stuck lying on the many nails in their lives. They are lying on the nails of their past; jobs that they hate, unhealthy relationships, bad decisions, toxic business partners, failing health, money issues, living conditions, and missed opportunities. The complainers just complain, and they rarely do anything else. They will not get a better diet, they will only complain about how they look and feel. They will not look for other opportunities to make more money, they will only complain about not having enough. They very seldom come up with solutions. We could all find something to complain about. The key is to do something about the issues in your life instead of only complaining about them.

To improve on your life and move yourself out of these categories, you need to complete the People Type exercises on page 198.

Chapter 10: Princess Does Not Live Here Anymore

"Bad habits are like chains that are too light to feel until they are too heavy to carry."

- Warren Buffet

I had a friend who at one point in her life was a crack addict, prostitute, and an exotic dancer. Her stage name was Princess. She later turned her life around, kicked the drug habit, left the streets, stopped dancing, and later earned Bachelor's, Master's, and Doctorate degrees. She said that one day after she had left that life behind, she was walking down the street and a guy walked up to her and said, "Princess?" She said that she looked at him and said, "I'm sorry, but Princess doesn't live here anymore."

To become the person you want to be, you must kick bad habits out of your house, the place which is symbolic of your life. When you get rid of those old habits, do not allow them in again. They will try to come in and eat and sleep with you. If you allow them in, before you know it, they will take over the entire house. This is why you often times see people who have lost weight a year later and they are heavier than they had ever been in their lives. There are people who have quit smoking, drinking, and using drugs who then allow those old habits to reenter their homes again. They become worse than they were before they quit. In recovery, it is referred to as relapsing.

As those old habits begin to occupy your home, no one else is welcome. Rational thinking is left out in the cold. Family members are also locked out, which is why the addict will steal from, and sometimes even hurt, his own family to take care of the habit. God is also gone. The addict becomes a different person.

Once you change your diet, start to eat healthy, and those cravings come, you have to look at that chocolate bar and say, "I am sorry, but she does not live here anymore." Once you give up your bad habits and drug and alcohol addictions, you must explain to your demons that your former self does not live there anymore. There will be leftovers in the kitchen, cookies in the pantry, and cinnamon buns at the mall that will begin to knock on your door again. You need to tell those nasty food demons that you are sorry, but she does not live here anymore. Explain to strife, laziness, dependency, and inadequacy that that person has moved to another location, a different address, and for all you know, she is dead. Help fear and rejection to understand that they are not welcomed. They can no longer take control over you. When doubt comes knocking, you need to tell her that the old you has left the building. You should never be subjected to any of those negative ideas, emotions, and habits again.

Values

To continue on the path of not being subjected to these negative ideas, emotions, and habits, you must permanently change your values. Carl Rogers said, "Clarifying your values is the essential first step to a richer, fuller, more productive life."

H. L Mencken said, "The one permanent emotion of the inferior man is fear - fear of the unknown, the complex, and the inexplicable. What he wants above everything else is safety."

At times, I have been afraid to take on certain challenges because I valued safety from failure and rejection more than accomplishing certain goals. As I peered in the future, I saw myself continuing to hold onto those values, never changing, never pursuing the goals in my life, never making important phone calls, and never even trying. Comfort felt better to me than having others think negatively of me. I was afraid to try because I was afraid to fail.

I wanted to write a book for years, but my fears kept me from trying. I was afraid to send it to an editor, afraid of mistakes that I had made, afraid that people who read it would not like it, and afraid that a publisher would not publish it. No one wants to fail, but you cannot put more value on not failing than on having success. If a surgeon values the fear of failure over success, he will never perform any operations. If a pilot values the fear of crashing more than the exhilaration of flying passengers to their destinations, he will never leave the runway.

We all want to feel good about ourselves and to be accepted by our peers. When our ideas are rejected, we feel like people are rejecting us. To achieve the success that you want, you will have to stop valuing safety and security more than achieving your goals and dreams. Your values need to be interconnected with the desired outcomes that you expect in your life. When this occurrence becomes evident, success can not and will not elude you.

Live on the Edge

When you change your values, you will not be afraid to make the necessary changes needed to get you to the place you want to go. You will not be afraid to live on the edge.

I was at a Florida State vs. University of Maryland basketball game during Maryland's 2002 National Championship season. I was court-side when a gentleman, who appeared to be the head of security, walked up to me and said, "I do not care if you cheer very loud. In fact, I want you to be crazy, yell at those Maryland players, fuss at the referees, and whatever else you must do to help us win. I want you to live on the edge; go right up to the line without crossing it and getting kicked out." I took his advice and did everything that I could, but we still lost. For us to beat that team, a lot of us would have probably had to cross the line.

Living on the edge means that you take more risks. To get to where you want to go in life, you will have to take more chances. Do not hurt people or break the law, but you have to do something that will make you stand out. If you do not live on the edge, then you will blend in with everyone else and become irrelevant. While at FSU playing football, we would go through rigorous training in the off-season. We were all supposed to wear the same uniform, including shoes, during our training. I wanted to do something to break the monotony of this intense training. I wanted to try something different. I went to my closet and pulled out my pink and green special edition Bo Diddley Nikes. The pink and green Nikes were a smash hit with all the players and the coaches. It not only built morale, but it allowed the group and I to skip a few drills. The coach said that because I had had the courage to wear them and they were different, to say the least, he was going to reward our entire group. Those shoes were the main topic of conversation that day and were requested several more times.

Living on the edge also means that you will be doing a little more than everyone else. Do not lag behind so that others can catch up. If they are not moving at your pace, then you must move on. They may not have the ambition or the drive that you have, and they will not receive the same rewards that you will. They could be on a different mission.

Heifer and the Ox, by Aesop

A heifer saw an ox hard at work harnessed to a plow, and tormented him with reflections on his unhappy fate in being compelled to labor. Shortly afterwards, at the harvest festival, the owner released the ox from his yoke, but bound the heifer with cords and led him away to the altar to be slain in honor of the occasion. The ox saw what was being done and said with a smile to the heifer: "For this you were allowed to live in idleness, because you were presently to be sacrificed."

Be careful if there is no one talking about you. The worse place to be is on a team where the coach never says anything to you. This is when you know that he does not think you have what it takes to play, or that you are just not coachable. Do not gloat in idleness. When the two year old is too quiet, you need to check on him because he is probably playing in the toilet.

I am a fanatic when it comes to watching shows like MTV Cribs. If you have any ambition, the way that these people live will make you sick to your stomach. You should use that sickness that you feel to dream about the possibilities of "what if." What if you could live that lifestyle? What do you need to do to get there? Is it possible? I say to you, yes it is. You can live the life you want. Those people are not special; they have just achieved some special and specific goals. Sitting there is not an option. Get up and go live your dreams.

For most, there are people fifteen minutes away from you who are living your dreams. There are people who are all around you who are in great relationships. There are people within a rocks throw of you who drive your dream car, live in your dream house, and have the career that you want. You just need to believe that it can happen to you and act accordingly.

Paul Orberson, former high school coach and founder of Fortune Hi-Tech Marketing, who became a multi-millionaire in network marketing as reported by Forbes Magazine, said, "We take ourselves too serious. We live as though if we fail that it will be the end of us."

Remember we must be like children. Children will try anything. They do not care how they look. Put a child in a chair and hold your hands out. They will jump rather recklessly in your arms with a smile. They run, play, and fall constantly. They do not worry about their clothes getting dirty. Their noses run constantly. They lose and break things, but they have fun. As we get older, we start to worry about how we look when we take chances. We start to worry about what others will think about us. We fail to remember that we are here for only a short time. When we say, "If I had only known then what I know now, then I would have…," many times what we are really saying is that we should have taken more chances.

I get hundreds of requests or more each year from young student athletes wanting advice about whether they should try to play a sport beyond high school. I say one hundred percent of the time that they should at least try. The reason is rather obvious to me. You do not want to get to the point where you physically cannot perform and say you wish you had attempted.

You must remember that you cannot value the fear of failure over succeeding. It may not be that others are better than you are. You may not have had the opportunity, received the proper training, or been placed in the right environment to succeed. So you should never be intimidated by anything or anyone. Eleanor Roosevelt said, "No one should make you feel inferior without your consent."

Even God does not have respect of persons. In other words, he does not play favorites. My dad used to have one question when we would bring a grade home that was less than perfect. He asked if there was anyone who made an A on the test or in the class. He would then say, "If anyone else can, you can also."

Hank Aaron said, "I never doubted my ability, but when you hear all your life you're inferior, it makes you wonder if the other guys have something you've never seen before. If they do, I'm still looking for it."

A man walks up to famous car maker Enzo Ferrari to express to him improvements that he thought could be made to his cars. Mr. Ferrari refuses to listen to him, brushing him off as just an old farmer. The man vows to get even and start his own car manufacturing company nearby Mr. Ferrari's company. The farmer's name was Ferruccio Lamborghini.

The feeling of inferiority is why certain challenges are not accepted and certain questions not asked. No boy wants to walk up to a pretty girl and be rejected. No businessperson wants to feel the rejection of investors. Even if the top prospect on your list does not invest in your company, that does not mean that you will not be successful.

A young entrepreneur got his coveted meeting with one of the most successful investors in the world. They talked for ten hours. The investor did not see his vision and wanted no part of the entrepreneur's type of business. He said that he could not see what the hype was all about. In fact, he told the young entrepreneur that those types of companies usually come and go. The young entrepreneur tried to get him to invest, but the investor wanted no part of it. The investor would later say that this was one of his biggest investing mistakes. The investor was billionaire Warren Buffet. The young entrepreneur was billionaire software pioneer Bill Gates.

These lessons teach us to keep moving in the face of it all. Do not stop when you have not achieved the results that you want, but rather, keep moving.

Everything has to be moving. Movement is life. Plants have to grow or they will die. Your heart has to continue beating. Blood has to continue to flow through your veins. If you place a rock in a stream, the stream will eventually win the battle because of its movement. Even the earth is continually moving. The earth rotates on its rotational axis.

It rotates once every twenty-four hours. It is moving at a rate of 1,000 miles per hour. The time it takes for the earth to rotate completely is called a day. The earth's rotation gives us night and day. As it rotates, it is in what is called an elliptical orbit around the sun. It takes roughly 365 days for the earth to go around the sun once. This means that the earth is rushing through space around the sun at a rate of about 67,000 miles per hour.

Your business must keep moving. When you start to rest on your laurels, you will begin to lose steam. When you lose steam, your zeal starts to go. When your zeal leaves, then the momentum is no longer present and that is when you, your company, or your relationship, is dead. You should always be expanding. It is always good to have new people with fresh new ideas that can help your cause.

Conrad Hilton said, "Success seems to be connected with action. Successful people keep moving."

Chapter 11: Your Health and You

"The greatest wealth is health."

-Virgil

Eat Healthy

Let me start by saying you should consult your physician before you start any diet or exercise program. I am not an expert in the field of health. However, what I do know about health is that you need a good dose of it to survive. I have always struggled with my weight. I have always been a person who has to fight the bad carbohydrate demons. I have never liked cardiovascular workouts and have only lifted weights in an effort to look better rather than for health reasons. Many people have this outside-in mentality when it comes to dealing with their health. It is evident by the increase in plastic and cosmetic surgery. More people will exercise and diet to look thin than to improve their health. That is fine as long as it serves both needs. However, it becomes detrimental when people develop eating disorders in their efforts or take inordinate amounts of drugs to gain weight and build muscle when most of those substances have never been tested to assess the long-term effects.

We all know that there seems to be a disease epidemic in this country, which sounds a bit redundant, but it seems as though more and more people are contracting diseases at a faster pace than ever before. With all of the technological advances that we have made, we should at least be able to slow the pace of this rapid spread of disease. Since we cannot solely depend on technology to keep us alive and healthy, we must go back to the basics of eating a proper diet and engaging in regular exercise.

Two of the top causes of death in this country are heart disease and cancer. Diet and physical exercise are both possible preventatives for these diseases. Cancer.org states that, "Increasingly, researchers agree that poor diets and sedentary lifestyles are among the most important contributors to cancer risk. We must maintain a healthy weight and make better food choices." It further states that we need at least five servings of vegetables and fruits a day, especially those with the most color because the color signifies a high nutrient content. It goes on to say that these foods are packed with vitamins, minerals, antioxidants, and many other substances that work together to lower the risk of several cancers, including cancers of the lung, mouth, esophagus, stomach, and colon. Not only that, but if prepared properly vegetables and fruits are usually low in calories, so eating them in place of higher-calorie foods can help you control your weight.

I needed to increase my intake of fruits and vegetables. I had never eaten enough of either until I was introduced to super fruits. These fruits are packed with most of the vital nutrients that we need on a daily basis. They are the acai berry, blueberry, cranberry, grape, guarana, mangosteen, noni, pomegranate, sea-buckthorn, and wolfberry (gogi). Some of these fruits have also been introduced as main ingredients in functional food beverages. These functional food beverages aid people in receiving vital nutrients. They are perfect for people with a lifestyle on the go who do not have time to peel the required servings of fruit each day.

Drink Plenty of Water

You should also engage in drinking plenty of water each day. Drinking water helps the body to metabolize stored fat. You should drink at least eight eight-ounce glasses of water each day. When you exercise, drink more water. Two thirds of our weight is made up of water. Our blood is around eighty-three percent water. Our muscles are seventy-five percent water. Our brain is seventy-four percent water and our bones are twenty-two percent water. Drinking water helps with a variety of issues; besides being great for your heart, water aids in digestion, detoxifying your kidneys and liver, and even in losing weight. Some symptoms of not drinking enough water are headaches and fatigue. You should drink water even before you are thirsty. I had a friend tell me that he gets all the water he needs in sweet tea. Please do not use this philosophy. You should replace the coffee, tea, sodas, and Kool-Aid type drinks for more water if you want your health to improve.

Exercise

Drinking water and eating healthy is great, but physical exercise is just as essential to improving your overall health. It substantially reduces the risk of developing cardiovascular disease, type-two diabetes, and certain cancers. You should perform physical exercise at least three to five times a week. It will lower blood pressure and cholesterol, slow the development and progression of osteoporosis, ease symptoms of arthritis, and keep you from being obese. It also will help your heart remain, or become, stronger and healthier. Your heart is the strongest muscle in your body, bringing oxygen-rich blood to all of your muscles and helping them work as hard as you do. It makes sense to keep your heart strong and healthy. It will ultimately make your whole body work more efficiently. Remember, your health is more important than anything that you can acquire or be. If you are not healthy to enjoy all of your success, then what is the point?

Quiet Time and Proper Rest

A couple of practices that are overlooked when it comes to taking care of one's self are spending time meditating or praying, and getting proper rest.

Every day before football practice in high school, our coach would make us lie on our backs and get what he called "quiet time." He said that the quiet time was to make us think about what we had to do for that day and assess how we could do it better.

You have to truly learn to like yourself. You spend more time with you than anyone else. People who take quiet time to think, pray, and plan are more successful than those who do not.

Some people cannot stand to be alone. They have to be doing something. They have to have chaos. They have to have the television on, or be surfing the internet, on their cell phones, stuffing their face with food, or participating in other frenzied activities. You have to take time for yourself and get proper rest or your body and mind will shut down. Sometimes with everything that is going on - spouses, kids, work, school, prospects, meetings, bills, projects - you can get caught up and never take time to get some rest. For some, the only way they will rest is if they are laid up in the hospital. More often than not, the doctor tells them that bed rest is what they need.

Do not wait until this happens. Slow down. I know you want to be a hard worker. That is perfectly fine. I know you are ready to hustle to make it happen, but remember you cannot do everything today. Your body needs to rest. Do not just keep filling your body up with a bunch of pills and caffeine to substitute for the rest you need. Ultimately, that type of lifestyle will catch up with you.

Chapter 12: How It Ends

"When I stand before God at the
end of my life,
I would hope that I would not have a
single bit of talent left, and could say
I used everything you gave me."

-Erma Bombeck

The Next You

There is always room for another star in your field. Just when you think that the market is saturated with stars in your field, another star comes along. There is always a star waiting in the wings. In 1986, a kid was just being born when Michael Jordan was tearing the league up with his highflying act. No one ever thought there would be anything close to him, as Hall of Fame sports commentator Dick Vitale later said. However, somewhere in Ohio was a little boy sucking on a bottle, eating mashed potatoes, and learning to walk. He would later have more hype entering the league than any basketball player in the history of the game. People would start referring to him as King. His name of course, is LeBron James.

I have a little exercise that I want you to perform. I want you to write down who or what has come before you in your field of endeavor. It could be a company after which you would like to pattern your company. It could be an actress, actor, entertainer, athlete, artist, inventor, or businessperson. When their name is mentioned, your name is mentioned. This section is for the huge dreamers. It is for people who think big. If you are not a huge dreamer, then you need to skip this exercise.

Are you the next superstar? Is your company the next big success story?

After writing your list, insert your name in the next space. Your list may be longer or shorter than what is below. Here are a few examples:

1. Bill Gates, Michael Dell

   —————

2. Michael Jordan, LeBron James

   —————

3. Aretha Franklin, Beyonce Knowles

   —————

4. Denzel Washington, Tom Cruise

   —————

5. My Space, YouTube

   —————

6. T. D. Jakes, Joel Osteen

   —————

7. Agatha Christie, Stephen King

   —————

8. ——————, ——————
   —————?

Pursuit of Happiness

The next "you" will help you in your quest to be the best that you can be. There is nothing wrong with aspiring to reach lofty goals. Even if you never reach your goals, you should at least pursue them. The Declaration of Independence states, "We hold these truths to be self-evident, that all men are created equal, that they are endowed by their creator certain unalienable rights, among those are Life, Liberty, and the Pursuit of Happiness."

People who do not pursue happiness are not in line with what the Creator wants for them. We were not created for constant sadness, sickness, and terrible relationships. There are people who have been feeling bad for so long that it just seems like a part of them. If you are to be and do more, you will have to start to think of yourself in a better light.

Many people are speeding down the road to nowhere. If you are one of those people not in hot pursuit of happiness, then you need to be stopped, arrested, and read your rights. Here is what you will hear: Stop! You are speeding on the road that leads to nowhere. You have the right to pursue happiness, you have been feeling bad for too long, and anything short of this is unjustified and unwarranted. If you give up your right, you will forever feel undeserving, unwanted, and unappreciated. You will have to spend a night in the jail of failure. The good news is that you will be released on your own recognizance after you sign a statement that says you will never travel on this road again.

Alexis de Tocqueville, an aristocratic Frenchman who came to the U.S. in 1831 when he was only twenty-five years old, studied our culture, practices, and attitudes. He later wrote in his book,

How It Ends

Democracy in America,

"The first thing that strikes me as a traveler in the United States is the innumerable multitude of those who seek to emerge from their original condition; and the second is the rarity of lofty ambition to be observed in the midst of the universally ambitious stir of society. No Americans are devoid of a yearning desire to rise, but hardly any appear to entertain hopes of great magnitude or to pursue very lofty aims. All are constantly seeking to acquire property power, and reputation; few contemplate these things upon a great scale; and this is the more surprising as nothing is to be discerned in the manners or laws of America to limit desire or to prevent it from spreading its impulses in every direction..."

You should go ahead and pursue what you want out of life. There is no crime against the pursuit, but rather the non-pursuit, of happiness. Therefore, you should only speed towards the happiness that you want and you must believe that it exists.

It is All Within Your Reach

In Russell Conwell's classic book, Acres of Diamonds, he tells the story of a rich farmer who learns of the largest diamond mine in the world. The farmer cannot resist trying to find it. He sells his farm, leaves his family, and spends all he has in his quest. Essentially, he goes searching for happiness. After searching all of his life with no luck, he tosses himself in a river and drowns.

The man who buys his farm is out in the back of the farm one day drinking out of the brook, when he looks down and sees something shining. He picks the object up, takes it home, and places it on his mantle. One day, a priest visiting him sees it and tells the farmer that it is the largest diamond he has ever seen. He then asks him where he got it. The farmer says he found it outside in the brook. The priest finally convinces the farmer to show him where he had found the shiny object. They go to the brook and find more of these shiny objects. It comes to be that the whole farm is sitting on the famed Diamond Mine of Golconda. It is the most magnificent diamond-mine in the history of mankind. There are literally acres of diamonds. As it turns out, the previous owner had searched the world over looking for something that was in his backyard.

While on your search for happiness, you must understand that what you need to reach the happiness you want is within you and/or all around you. You need to know and understand that it is all inside. You do not have to blindly move to another city or have someone else's talent, background, looks, or intelligence. You only need to walk into the understanding that you possess all that you need. Yes, you will see it when you believe it. You will come across every opportunity that you need to make you a success.

Interestingly enough, when people look back on their lives, they usually do not wish that they were someone else. They do not think about how and where they were born. They only think about the opportunities they have missed. Your squandered opportunities, wasted talent, and those great ideas represent your acres of diamonds. There are still acres of diamonds around you today that you have not discovered. You need to make sure that you are not looking all over the place for something that you have in your hands. It is true that sometimes you cannot see the forest for the trees. Even if you have missed previous opportunities, there is no need for you to miss new ones.

You must be willing to start over if you are going to discover the acres of diamonds that are in your life today. You must be willing to forgive and be forgiven. Forgiveness is the highest form of starting over because it means that you are accepting responsibility for those outcomes, and you are willing to begin again.

No one has had to start over more times than dieters or people who have terrible habits. Mark Twain said, "Giving up smoking is the easiest thing that I've ever done because I done it thousands of times." Sometimes you just have to say that is it and start over again tomorrow. I would have been done years ago if I were not able to start again. That is why forgiveness is so important because it allows you to start over with yourself and with God. To really use forgiveness as a point to start over, you must actually be sorry for your actions. Martin Luther King, Jr. said, "Forgiveness shouldn't be an occasional act, but rather a permanent attitude." Sir Elton John sings a song titled, Sorry Seems to Be the Hardest Word. For many people, saying I am sorry is difficult. For me, it has always been difficult.

I remember being in kindergarten, swinging on a swing, when a girl walked in front of me and I accidentally kicked her in the nose. Her nose began to bleed and she started to cry. I felt bad for her. That was until the teacher told me that I had to apologize. I was distraught. It was a difficult time. I remember the feeling in my gut that I had that day. I did not want to apologize because I did not feel like I had done anything wrong. It is always hard to say you are sorry whether you are wrong or not. It appears that you are accepting blame. No one likes to admit that they were wrong. Steve Martin said, "An apology? Bah! Disgusting! Cowardly! Beneath the dignity of any gentleman, however wrong he might be."

When you do not apologize, it not only hinders you in your current relationships, but it also hampers future relationships. This non-forgiving attitude keeps you attached to the past. This is why you may leave one relationship and then be attracted to the same type of person in subsequent relationships. Like always attracts like. Christian Ponder said that when you do not forgive, you remain attached to the past. When Jesus went to the cross, he was speaking about his crucifiers when he said, "Father, forgive them; for they know not what they do." Jesus used forgiveness to detach himself from the seemingly selfish acts of his detractors. He understood that his life held a bigger mission and purpose. He was not about to remain attached to any hate during his final hours of mortality.

You cannot live your life never trusting or believing in anyone because of what has happened in your past. The one thing that I learned from my deceased younger brother is that you must believe in people. We go through life seeing advertisements and knowing that some fine print tells the rest of the story. We have come to expect that the car salesman will always say that someone was just in earlier to buy the car that we are test-driving. We know that the introductory APR will get us into trouble with credit card companies. We understand that there is a catch to sending our name in for a chance at winning the sweepstakes. We have to ask ourselves if there really is a free iPod waiting for us to claim when we open that email attachment.

We grow up listening to our parents tell us not to swear and then we find out that they do. Our boss lies to us, saying that there is not enough money in the budget to give us a raise, only for us to learn that a position was created for his friend making twice as much as we already do. Our spouses and kids disappoint us. We are never appreciated for the things we do, only ridiculed for the things that we do not do. All of these instances help to stack the deck against trust. All you believe is that everyone else is playing the cards of disloyalty. Therefore, when we hear about internet millionaires, people who have made fortunes selling items on eBay, in real estate, or multilevel marketing, there is no wonder we are skeptical. We see couples getting married and say that they just do not know what they are getting into. We question everything that we see, not to mention that which we do not. Our faith in God is easily shaken to the point that we question His very existence. We give up too quickly. We are slow to smile, hesitant to speak, and afraid to lend a helping hand all because we do not trust anyone or anything.

Even in all of this, do not give up on hope. Do not give up on the impossible. Oprah said, "God can dream a dream bigger for you than you can dream for yourself." It can happen. It is possible. Isaiah 40:4 says, "Every valley shall be exalted... the crooked places made straight…" There are good people who will help you. It is not all a fraud. Everyone is not out to get you.

I have had the hardest time with this. I must say that I became a bitter person towards everyone and everything after getting used many times. I did not trust anyone. Furthermore, I took pride in explaining to people why I did not trust them. However, you must understand that there are people who have good hearts and clean thoughts. There are those who would like to see you succeed. Find them and trust again. Start to believe again. Stop worrying and start acting on the dreams that remain in your heart. You must rid yourself of the negative thoughts of the naysayers. Those negative thoughts cloud your vision. Your acres of diamonds are all around you. It is up to you to do whatever it takes to find them. You must believe that it is possible. Impossible really reads I'm Possible. I am able. I Can.

Sick and Tired

From this day forward, you should start to operate on the premise that it is possible. You need to head toward your dreams. Detach yourself from the failures of the past and attach yourself to the dreams of the future.

Fannie Lou Hamer was born October 6, 1917, in Montgomery County, Mississippi. She was the granddaughter of a slave and the youngest of twenty children. Her parents were sharecroppers. Sharecropping, or "halfing," as it was sometimes called, was a system of farming whereby workers were allowed to live on a plantation in return for working the land. When the crop was harvested, they would split the profits in half with the plantation owner. Sometimes the owner would pay for the seed and fertilizer, but usually the sharecropper paid those expenses out of his half. It was a hard way to make a living and sharecroppers generally were born poor, lived poor, and died poor.

At age six, Fannie Lou began helping her parents in the cotton fields. By the time she was twelve, she was forced to drop out of school and work full time to help support her family. Once grown, she married another sharecropper named Perry "Pap" Hamer.

In 1962, members of the SNCC (Student Non-Violent Coordinating Committee) came to her town and held a voter registration meeting. This was the first time that she had heard that African Americans had a constitutional right to vote. At that point, she decided she had had enough of sharecropping. She left her home on August 31, 1962, and took seventeen others with her to the courthouse to register to vote. While on their way home they were stopped, arrested, jailed, and beaten. The plantation owner paid her a visit after she was released from jail. He explained to her that if she insisted on voting and trying to get others to do the same, she would have to leave his plantation. She had been there for eighteen years. The plantation was all that she knew.

She thought about what he had said to her and decided that his statement would be the turning point in her life. She decided to make a change. She said, "I'm sick and tired of being sick and tired." With the increased feeling of sickness, she felt that she had to leave the plantation that very same day. She became an activist and was very instrumental in the Voting Rights Act being passed.

You have to get to the point where you are sick and tired of being sick and tired. You have to become sick of your cesspool. You have to become sick of living from hand to mouth. You have to become sick of being stepped on. You have to become sick of being mistreated. Only when people are sick and tired of getting what they have been getting will they do something to get something different. You should know that insanity is doing the same thing over and over again and expecting different results.

Getting There

When you are sick of what you have been getting, then you can get on the right tracks and move in the right direction to where you want to go. The key is not only being on the right tracks, but also heading in the right direction. You can be on the right tracks headed in the wrong direction and still get run over by the train. So being on the right tracks headed in the right direction will be the key to you "getting there." "There" is your place in life that will manifest success.

When you are headed "there," you will become less anxious. You will be less dependent on others to make you feel important. You will know the difference between anxiety and urgency. You will be able to perform under stringent deadlines. You will understand that certain events do not complete your life, i.e., having kids, making a certain amount of money, living in a certain neighborhood, being a certain size or weight. Although these are some of the things that we strive for and continue to hope and dream for, they should not define you.

As you head "there," you worry less about what others think of you. You do not need attention. You make decisions based on what you feel is best for you and your family and not for others. You are not attached to the best deal. You become less obsessed with the way things need to be. You become less concerned about winning arguments. You are able to forgive others even if they have not forgiven you. You become more of a giver. You get more out of giving than receiving. You enter relationships asking others what you can do for them instead of trying to see what they can do for you. You shoot for higher goals and dreams with little or no thought of failing. You understand that failure is a part of the process. You understand that perfection does not exist and that trying is the first step to attainment. You are less likely to criticize. You distance yourself from the ---------------- negative ---------------- . You take quiet time to yourself and become more health conscious. You start to rest instead of just sleeping. Your belief level soars through the roof. Now you are "there."

When you get "there," you are able to give up your attachments, and become more and do more than you ever have before. There will not be any more caus'ing, if'ing, when'ing, don'ing, gon'ing, waiting, soon'ing, thinking, or complaining.

You will make things happen in life. You will follow through on what you start. You will finish what you begin. You will close what you open. You will tie up all the loose ends. You will begin to be honest with yourself first. You will keep promises that you make to yourself and others. You will get rid of the old person. You will not sit back and allow things to happen to you. You will never quit or give in. You will not be afraid of challenges. Your life will be transformed. People will not recognize you. The old you will be dead. The little things in life will not affect you. You will commit to it and be motivated through it. You will hustle to make it happen. Your fears will be there, but they will not paralyze you anymore. You will be ready to live on the edge. You will choose people who can help you and everyone else will be out of your life. Your negative activities will become positive events. These events will uplift and inspire you. You will look for and find your higher calling in life. You will no longer drift, watch the clock, or make ruts. You will make mistakes, but they will be full speed ahead. You may fail, but your conviction will remain.

Taking out the garbage no longer bothers you. Your chaotic house no longer hinders you. The past no longer haunts you. The future no longer scares you. Instead of sitting in yesterday, you stand in tomorrow. You are one with yourself and your Creator. You now know that you are here for a reason. You no longer worry about loved ones who have passed on. You understand that they were so special that God needed them there more than you needed them here. You now understand that problems will still arise, but you will handle them. Some tears may still come, but you will be able to get through the crisis. Now you can switch gears with ease. Your vengeance is gone. You are sick and tired of being sick and tired. Now it is time to live it, breathe it, and be it. It is time to seal the deal, close the curtains, end the show, and finish what you started and ultimately make it happen. Ultimately, you walk into the understanding that everything that you need or want is inside and all around you.

How it Ends

At the beginning of this book, I expressed the notion that everything has to start with God. Now you have come to the end and you must understand that more importantly, everything has to end with God. When you die, you must meet God again to be judged. God is the author and finisher of our faith. He is the beginning and the end. He is Alpha and Omega.

Mark 8:36 says, "What shall it profit a man, if he shall gain the whole world, and lose his own soul." The material things that this book has helped you to acquire will not and cannot go with you. You will not be able to take your homes, clothes, Blackberries, money, laptops, cars, iPods, iPhones, land, businesses, or anything else with you. Thus, this stuff is only stuff that you have, but it is not really yours. Your spirit is all that will go. It is what will be with you forever. You are not here for long. What should you really cherish the most? You can get everything that you want in and out of life: the cars, the house of your dreams, meet and marry your soul mate, and have a fulfilling career, but if you do not have a relationship with God, you will always feel empty inside.

Remember what Dr. Mike Murdock said, "God has not created a world in which he wouldn't be needed in." All the stuff in the middle becomes a mirage if you do not understand from where it comes. The only thing that will live forever is what you put in your heart, mind, and soul. Stay focused, always believe in the impossible, and one day your dreams will intersect God's plans for your life and success will be inevitable. It is coming. You feel it. You know it. You see it. You deserve it. You believe it. You are it. The moment is here and it is now.

May peace be unto you and thanks to our Lord and savior Jesus Christ.

People Types Workbook

This exercise should be used to help an individual or team complete goals and meet objectives. It can be completed by individuals, families, businesses, organizations, groups, or teams.

Causers

Goal:_____

Date:_____

What have you, your family, company, team, etc., been Caus'ing about up until this point? Write down your Causes. For example, Cause I...; Cause he...; Cause a particular situation...; Cause I do not have the money..., etc.

1. Cause

_____

_____

_____

2. Cause

_____

_____

_____

3. Cause

_____

_____

_____

4. Cause

_____

_____

_____

5. Cause

_____

_____

_____

6. Cause

_____

_____

_____

7. Cause

_____

7. Cause *(cont.)*

_____

_____

What are some steps you need to take to stop Caus'ing or to get rid of those Causes?

1.

_____

_____

_____

2.

_____

_____

_____

3.

_____

_____

_____

4.

_____

_____

_____

5.

_____

_____

_____

What are some other issues and solutions that you need to work on to eliminate the Caus'ing?

_____

_____

_____

_____

_____

_____

_____

_____

_____

_____

Wheners

Goal:_____

Date:_____

What have you, your family, company, team, etc., been When'ing about up until this point? Write down your Whens. For example: When I...; When he...; When she...; When we launch our marketing campaign...; When we make more money...; When I get my income tax...; When my children are older..., etc.

1. When

_____

_____

_____

2. When

_____

_____

_____

3. When

_____

_____

_____

4. When

_____

_____

_____

5. When

_____

_____

_____

6. When

_____

_____

_____

7. When

_____

_____

_____

What steps do you need to take so that When'ing does not stop you from completing your goals?

1.

2.

3.

4.

5.

_____

_____

_____

What are some other issues and solutions that you need to work on so that you will eliminate the When'ing?

_____

_____

_____

_____

_____

_____

_____

_____

_____

_____

_____

_____

_____

_____

_____

_____

Sooners

Goal:_____

Date:_____

What have you, your family, company, team, etc., been Soon'ing
about up until this point. Write down your Soon'ing statements.
For example: As Soon as I…; As Soon as they…; As Soon as my
husband…; As Soon as our finances change…, etc.

1. Soon (as)

_____

_____

_____

2. Soon (as)

_____

_____

_____

3. Soon (as)

_____

_____

_____

4. Soon (as)

_____

_____

_____

5. Soon (as)

_____

_____

_____

6. Soon (as)

_____

_____

_____

7. Soon (as)

_____

_____

_____

What steps do you need to take so that Soon'ing does not stop you from completing your goals?

1.

_____

_____

_____

2.

_____

_____

_____

3.

_____

_____

_____

4.

_____

_____

_____

5.

_____

_____

_____

What are some other issues and solutions that you need to work on so that you will eliminate the Soon'ing?

_____

_____

_____

_____

_____

_____

_____

_____

_____

_____

_____

_____

_____

_____

Donors

Goal:_____

Date:_____

What have you, your company, family, team, etc., been Don'ing about up until this point. Write down your Don'ing statements. For example: I Do not know the interest rate on my credit cards...; We Do not know what the status of our long term investments...; I Do not know how much my accountant makes...; I Do not care how much it cost as long as I can afford the monthly payments...; I Do not know how much I pay my agent..., etc.

1. Do not

_____

_____

_____

2. Do not

_____

_____

_____

3. Do not

_____

_____

3. Do not (cont.)

_____

4. Do not

_____

_____

_____

5. Do not

_____

_____

_____

6. Do not

_____

_____

_____

7. Do not

_____

_____

_____

What steps do you need to take so that Don'ing does not stop you from completing your goals?

1.

_____

_____

_____

2.

_____

_____

_____

3.

_____

_____

_____

4.

_____

_____

_____

5.

_____

_____

_____

What are some other issues and solutions that you need to work so that you will eliminate the Don'ing?

_____

_____

_____

_____

_____

_____

_____

_____

_____

_____

_____

_____

_____

_____

_____

_____

Ifers

Goal:_____

Date:_____

What have you, your company, family, team, etc., been If'ing about. For example: If I had more money...; If they would give us an opportunity...; If we were in the right location..., etc.

1. If

_____

_____

_____

2. If

_____

_____

_____

3. If

_____

_____

_____

4. If

_____

_____

_____

5. If

_____

_____

_____

6. If

_____

_____

_____

7. If

_____

_____

_____

What steps do you need to take so that If'ing does not stop you from completing your goals?

1.

_____

_____

_____

2.

_____

_____

_____

3.

_____

_____

_____

4.

_____

_____

_____

5.

_____

_____

_____

What are some other issues and solutions that you need to work
on so that you eliminate the If'ing?

_____

_____

_____

_____

_____

_____

_____

_____

_____

_____

_____

_____

_____

_____

_____

Goners

Goal:_____

Date:_____

What have you, your family, company, team, etc., been Gon'ing about up until this point. Write down your Gon'ing statements. For example: I'm Going to...; Our business is Going to...; Our team is Going to..., fixing to..., gonna..., about to..., etc.

1. Going to

_____

_____

_____

2. Going to

_____

_____

_____

3. Going to

_____

_____

_____

4. Going to

_____

_____

_____

5. Going to

_____

_____

_____

6. Going to

_____

_____

_____

7. Going to

_____

_____

_____

What steps do you need to take so that Gon'ing does not stop you from completing your goals?

1.

2.

3.

4.

5.

_____

_____

_____

What are some other issues and solutions that you need to work on to eliminate the Gon'ing?

_____

_____

_____

_____

_____

_____

_____

_____

_____

_____

_____

_____

_____

Waiters

Goal:_____

Date:_____

What have you, your family, company, team, etc., been Waiting on. For example: Wait until we get our credit repaired...; Wait until I get my gym membership...; Wait until we come up with a title for our album..., etc.

1. Wait

_____

_____

_____

2. Wait

_____

_____

_____

3. Wait

_____

_____

_____

4. Wait

_____

_____

_____

5. Wait

_____

_____

_____

6. Wait

_____

_____

_____

7. Wait

_____

_____

_____

What steps do you need to take to stop Waiting or to not be a Waiter any longer?

1.

_____

_____

_____

2.

_____

_____

_____

3.

_____

_____

_____

4.

_____

_____

_____

5.

_____

_____

_____

What are some other issues and solutions that you need to work
on to eliminate the Waiting?

_____

_____

_____

_____

_____

_____

_____

_____

_____

_____

_____

_____

_____

_____

Complainers

Goal:_____

Date:_____

What have you, your family, company, team, etc., been complaining about. Write down all the complaints that you have about your business, coworkers, spouse, etc.

1. Complaint

_____

_____

_____

2. Complaint

_____

_____

_____

3. Complaint

_____

_____

_____

4. Complaint

_____

_____

_____

5. Complaint

_____

_____

_____

6. Complaint

_____

_____

_____

7. Complaint

_____

_____

_____

What steps do you need to take so that Complaining does not stop you from completing your goals?

1.

_____

_____

_____

2.

_____

_____

_____

3.

_____

_____

_____

4.

_____

_____

_____

5.

_____

_____

_____

What are some other issues and solutions that you need to work
on to eliminate the Complaining?

_____

_____

_____

_____

_____

_____

_____

_____

_____

_____

_____

_____

_____

_____

_____

Thinkers

What have you, your family, company, team, etc., been Thinking about. Write down what you have been Thinking about. For example: I have been thinking about starting my own business...; I have been thinking about writing a book...; Our company has been thinking about doing some major advertising..., etc.

1. (I am) Thinking about

_____

_____

_____

2. (We are) Thinking of

_____

_____

_____

3. Think

_____

_____

_____

4. Think

_____

_____

_____

5. Think

_____

_____

_____

6. Think

_____

_____

_____

7. Think

_____

_____

_____

What steps do you need to take so that just Thinking does not stop you from completing your goals?

1.

_____

_____

_____

2.

_____

_____

_____

3.

_____

_____

_____

4.

_____

_____

_____

5.

_____

_____

_____

What are some other issues and solutions that you need to work on for you not to just Think, but rather to make some decisions and take action?

_____

_____

_____

_____

_____

_____

_____

_____

_____

_____

_____

_____

_____

_____

_____

Finishers

What do you, your family, company, team, etc., need to finish? What project or assignment do you need to focus on today? What have you started, but have not finished? It could be paying off a bill, organizing your garage, closing an account, satisfying a huge debt, filing important court documents, etc.

1. I need to Finish

_____

_____

_____

2. Our company needs to Finish

_____

_____

_____

3. As a family, we need to Finish

_____

_____

_____

4. Our organization needs to Finish

_____

_____

_____

5. Our Church needs to Finish

_____

_____

_____

6. Finish

_____

_____

_____

7. Finish

_____

_____

_____

What are some steps you need to take to Finish your goal(s)?

1.

_____

_____

_____

2.

_____

_____

_____

3.

_____

_____

_____

4.

_____

_____

_____

5.

_____

_____

_____

What are some other issues and solutions that you need to work on in order for you, your company, or your team to Finish goals?

_____

_____

_____

_____

_____

_____

_____

_____

_____

_____

_____

_____

_____

_____

_____

About the Author

Kendrick Scott is an author, speaker, trainer, and personal coach. He is President and C.E.O. of Kendrick Scott and Associates Communications Company, LLC., which specializes in the development of individuals, businesses, and teams, helping them to achieve optimum results.

Kendrick is from Chiefland, Florida, a small town in northwest Florida. He graduated from Chiefland High School and later attended Florida State University where he earned his Bachelor's in Political Science and his Master's in Interdisciplinary Social Science with an emphasis in Public Administration.

He was a member of legendary Coach Bobby Bowden's 1st National Championship Football Team. As a senior, he was voted a Permanent Team Captain by his teammates.

For information on speaking engagements, coaching, and book signings please visit us at:

www.psychoticspeaker.com

email: kscott@psychoticspeaker.com

ph: 850-997-4686 • fx: 850-997-2113

toll free (877)-813-0655

Kendrick Scott & Associates
Communications Company, LLC
400 Capital Circle SE Suite 18192
Tallahassee, FL 32301-3839